SOLDIER C

BLUE ON BLUE

SOLDIER OF FORTUNE 7

BLUE ON BLUE

Tony Williams

For Charlotte and Amy

Arms consultants: Artemis,
London

First published in Great Britain 1995
22 Books, Invicta House, Sir Thomas Longley Road,
Rochester, Kent

Copyright © 1995 by 22 Books

The moral right of the author has been asserted

A CIP catalogue record for this book is available from the
British Library

ISBN 1 898125 35 X

10 9 8 7 6 5 4 3 2 1

Typeset by Hewer Text Composition Services, Edinburgh
Printed in Great Britain by Cox and Wyman Limited, Reading

1

The phone call came through to Colonel James Valin's apartment in Eaton Square. It was short and succinct. Sir Hadley Bryant-Marshall wished to see him for lunch the next day at his club in St James's. One o'clock precisely. There were no reasons given, and when Valin replaced the receiver he smelt the scent of war in the air and nodded in a satisfied fashion.

Valin arrived at the club at exactly the appointed time. The November weather was fiercely cold, with gusts of strong wind that carried flurries of icy rain and threatened to tear from his hand the large, black umbrella he used to shelter him from the cab to the door of the club. The doorman relieved him of the brolly, his British warm overcoat and trilby, and hung them all neatly behind the reception desk. Valin was tall and wore a grey soft-flannel double-breasted suit, striped shirt and regimental tie. His shoes were as shiny as the moment he'd left his flat, despite the arctic weather outside.

'I'm lunching with Sir Hadley Bryant-Marshall,'

he said to the receptionist. 'The name's Valin. Colonel James.'

The receptionist looked at Valin's military figure, and up at his face, ruddy from the wind outside and marred only by the livid scar that ran from forehead to cheek.

'You're expected, sir,' he said, and summoned a bell-boy to show the visitor to the dining-room.

Sir Hadley Bryant-Marshall was already at a secluded table beside one of the tall, rain-streaked windows that looked down on St James's Square, where a few chilled figures were hurrying for warmth and shelter.

He rose as the bell-boy showed Valin to his seat, and stuck out his hand.

'James,' he said. 'Good to see you. It's been a long time. Too long.'

'Sir Hadley,' replied Valin, and took the proffered hand, before they both sat.

'I took the liberty of ordering you a pink gin,' said Bryant-Marshall. 'Still your tipple, I hope.'

'Of course,' said Valin. 'Old habits, you know.'

'And I chose the meal. Potted shrimps, steak-and-kidney pie, and bread-and-butter pudding. It's the only thing to have here. Plus, of course, a bottle of something red. Is that to your liking?'

'It's your club, Hadley. You know the chef.'

'I should do. I got him the job. He was made redundant from the old regiment. Looked like he was going to end up sleeping rough on the

Embankment. I couldn't have that, so I got him a post here. Best steak-and-kidney man in the whole bloody British army. What's left of it.'

'Don't start me on that, Hadley,' said Valin. 'Or else we'll be here all day.'

As they ate and drank, they engaged in small talk, and it was only when coffee, brandy and port had arrived on the table, and cigars were lit, that the conversation turned to business.

'I hear you excelled yourself down in South America this summer. Put on a good show,' said Bryant-Marshall.

'We managed. But we left some good men down there.'

'Your young lieutenant. O'Rourke, isn't it?'

'That's correct. He's up in Norfolk, looking after my place there.'

'And your sergeant? The German?'

Valin shook his head. 'He didn't make it.'

'I'm sorry. How about the American? Spenser?'

Valin smiled a rare smile. 'He took a round, but we got him out. He married a girl we brought out too. They're living with her father in New York. There was only one other survivor. Another American. Angel. A good man. Young. Non-com material. He's somewhere on the West Coast, living the life of Riley, so I believe.'

'And you, James. What about you?'

'Surviving.'

'Anything on the horizon?'

3

Valin shook his head.

'You know what I'm involved in now?' asked Bryant-Marshall.

'Now that MI6 doesn't have the Soviets to worry about?'

'That's right.'

'No.'

'I've been seconded to the Home Office. Big desk. Big staff.'

'Sounds interesting.'

'Not bad. Pays the stud fees. Anyway, something's come up. Something in your line.'

'Like what?'

'Lord Petersham. Heard of him?'

'Certainly. Textiles, isn't it?'

'That's correct.'

'What about him?'

'He has a daughter. Fine-looking filly. Name of Vanessa.'

'Yes.'

'Ever heard of Lochnercrag?'

'No.'

'It's an island off the east coast of Scotland. Outside our territorial waters by a whisper.'

Valin said nothing.

'Heard of Dirk Robertson?'

'Is this *Twenty Questions*?'

'Bear with me. Have you?'

'The name rings a bell.'

'It should do. The man's a bloody billionaire.

4

Computer software. Got the Yanks beaten by a mile. Cleaned up in the eighties. He started at twenty-one, writing programmes in his mother's kitchen in Glasgow. By the time he was thirty he was earning half the national debt every year. Strange young fella. Got it into his head he's chieftain of his clan. A laird or some such nonsense. Anyway, Lochnercrag came up for sale and he bought it. He's got the place fortified like a bloody war zone. He even runs a private army up there. All strictly legal, of course. There's nothing that we, the government, can do about it. He can spend his money on any damn-fool thing he wants to. But it seems he's gone a bit too far.'

'How so?'

'Vanessa, the Petershams' girl. Robertson met her at a party on the mainland a few months ago. Took a shine to her. Invited her to visit his island. And now he won't let her go home. He's got the idea that he wants to marry her. Petersham is going mad.'

'What have you done about it so far?'

'Asked him nicely. He demurred. Threatened him with the law. He laughed. Says *he's* the law on Lochnercrag.'

'Send in the army.'

'Too messy. Robertson's men are loyal. The place is a bloody citadel. No, it wouldn't work. Anyway, the PM won't hear of it. We were thinking of recruiting some private ...' He didn't finish the sentence.

'Muscle.' Valin did it for him.

'Precisely,' said Bryant-Marshall, and poured himself some more port.

'Like me and my men.'

'Correct. Petersham isn't short of a bob or two. He'll pay.'

'How much?'

'A million sterling.'

'Nice round figure.'

'That's the only way to do business.'

'What's the layout? What's the strength of this private army of his?'

Bryant-Marshall leant down and brought up to the table a slim briefcase from the floor by his chair. 'All in here, James,' he said. 'Our full intelligence on the state of play on Lochnercrag. Plus a profile of the main players. You might know one or two of them.'

'How many men will it take?'

'That's up to you. Ten. A dozen maybe.'

'How do we get there?'

'Submarine. The PM *has* authorized that. Then a couple of rubber powerboats. The only problem is the weather. This winter seems to have set in early. It's not going to be a picnic. What do you say?'

'Not so fast, Hadley. I need to think about it. Study the data in there,' said Valin, gesturing at the briefcase.

'I'm afraid we need a decision quickly, James.

You're not the only fish in the sea, if you'll excuse the expression under the circumstances.'

'I need to speak to my men. How long has the girl been on the island?'

'Three weeks. She went for two days.'

'I can let you know my decision tomorrow. Is that soon enough?'

'Capital, James.' Bryant-Marshall took a card from his wallet and gave it to Valin. 'This is my direct line. Call me in the morning.'

Valin slipped the card in his top pocket.

2

After lunch Valin went straight back to his flat with the briefcase, and when he was comfortably seated with a whisky and soda, opened it.

Inside was a map of Lochnercrag, a thick bundle of glossy photographs of the place, and a pile of typed sheets of paper. The island was small, with cliffs on three sides and on the leeward a natural harbour. The cliffs were high and bleak, and the harbour, which had been improved with man-made jetties, was overlooked by some kind of concrete blockhouse with gun slits for windows. On the day the photos were taken, two large, luxurious-looking motor cruisers and a small yacht were moored in the harbour. On top of the cliffs was a helipad, also overlooked by a blockhouse. Inland, in a natural valley, were the main living quarters: a house for Dirk Robertson, with several outbuildings, and a fortress cum garrison for his troops. They seemed to number around fifty, and from the list of ordnance that came with the map, were heavily armed with the latest, state-of-the-art weaponry. Their leader was someone with a name familiar to Valin, and he pulled a wry face as he read the profile supplied.

The man's name was Roland Stone, a one-time major in the US Marines, who had fought with great valour in Vietnam, and had received the Congressional Medal of Honor plus three purple hearts for his pains. Valin had met the man in south-east Asia, and had liked him. Stone was a maverick, a renegade who treated his high command with the contempt that both he and Valin felt they deserved. He was the last person Valin wanted to face in a fire-fight on unknown territory.

Next he read the details of Dirk Robertson himself. He was, as Bryant-Marshall had told him, a self-made man. A boy who had left school at fifteen, bought a second-hand computer and learnt within hours everything there was to know about it and its programmes. He'd then gone on and taught himself to write software of his own which even a computer-illiterate could master within a few minutes. They'd caught on quickly, and before long, money was streaming into the headquarters of Robertson's company in Glasgow.

Within a few years of starting in business, Robertson had sold out to an American company in Silicon Valley. Then he simply started up again, ignoring the law suits that the US company brought against him. Five years after that, he sold out once again, to a rival company of the first. But this time he got a percentage of the profit on every programme sold that he had invented. According to the Inland Revenue, his income for the previous tax year had been something in the region of £20 million.

Nice work if you can get it, thought Valin, as he turned to the profiles of the others on the island.

Lady Vanessa Petersham was twenty-five. She'd been educated at Roedean and Cambridge, from which she graduated with a first-class honours degree in history. Then she'd joined the BBC as a researcher, had been promoted to assistant producer, and was just about to start on her first solo production, a documentary on rave culture in the UK.

Probably just as well she was kidnapped, thought Valin as he set aside the rest of the profiles and reached for the phone.

His first call was to Norfolk. Mark O'Rourke, Valin's second in command, answered it on the third ring. 'I think we might be on to a runner,' said Valin without preamble.

'You want me down?' O'Rourke was equally terse.

'Now,' said Valin, and put down the phone. Next he got out his battered Filofax and made two calls to America. Over there it was morning, and Carmen Spenser answered the phone when the first call, to New York, connected.

10

'Colonel!' she exclaimed, when he announced himself. 'How are you?'

'Well,' replied Valin. 'Yourself?

'Never better.'

'And your father?'

'In good health. Though he is still sad about the loss of the rest of our family.' Her father, Jesús Delgado, had left his wife, two daughters and a son dead in Colombia when he and his remaining daughter had come out after assisting Valin and his men on their last mission.

'And you, Carmen?' asked Valin. 'How are you coping?'

'I miss my family, but now I have Chris.' Chris Spenser, a Vietnam vet who toted a 6000 rounds per minute, 7.62-calibre electric-powered rotary Gatling mini gun, known as the M134, which he had used to great effect in South America, had fallen in love with the exotic Colombian beauty and married her at the culmination of the mission.

'Is he being good to you?' asked Valin.

'No one has ever been better.'

'Is he there?'

'Sure. He's just cooking brunch.'

'Sounds like you've tamed him.'

'We'll see . . . A moment.' And she was gone.

The next voice was male, with a languid American accent. 'Colonel,' said Chris Spenser. 'How are you today?'

11

'All the better for talking to you, Chris. And your lovely wife, of course.'

'You leave her alone. She's spoken for. I know what you silver-tongued Brits can do to women.'

'I'm flattered.' Then Valin changed the subject. 'How are you fixed, Chris?'

'Earning a few dollars bodyguarding.'

'Fancy a trip to freezing England. Well, Scotland in fact.'

'A job?'

'Yes.'

'In England.'

'Like I said, Scotland to be precise. In fact, to be even more precise, a small island just off the coast.' He went on to explain the mission, and the individuals concerned.

'Roland Stone,' said Spenser. 'Hell of a guy.'

'Know him?'

'Only by reputation.'

'Well, if you come, it's possible you'll get to know him very well indeed.'

'What's the pay, Colonel?'

'One million sterling, to be split equally among us.'

'How many of us?'

'So far, just me and O'Rourke. I'm going to call Angel the minute I put down the phone. But I should imagine ten or twelve.'

'Angel. Christ, he was in town a few weeks ago.

He took us all out to dinner. I've never seen so much alcohol.'

'He's well, then.'

'Blooming. Give him my regards.'

'So what about it, Chris?'

'Hey, Colonel. What do you think? I've had my uniform packed since we got home. Let's just try and keep the party as small as possible. I could use a tenth of a million ... What do you call them? Quid?'

'That's right.'

'Can you get me a decent gun?'

'A Gatling?'

'Sure. I believe your customs people wouldn't welcome me bringing my own.'

'Can do. There'll be a ticket waiting for you at Tower Travel on Broadway, tomorrow morning.'

'Hey, Colonel. Do me a favour, huh? Make it two. Where I go these days, Carmen goes. Better still, make it three. I've been promising Jesús a trip to merry old England all summer long.'

'November is hardly holiday time.'

'Life's a holiday.'

'Then pack some winter woollies, it's cold over here.'

'And very little central heating as I remember.'

'Don't worry, Chris, I'll get you booked into an American hotel. As much heat and ice for your drinks as you can manage.'

'Sounds good. See you in London.'

The next call, to California, was answered by a young-sounding woman. 'Johnny Angelo, please,' said Valin.

'He's asleep right now.'

'Then wake him up, please.'

'I'm afraid he doesn't like being woken this early.'

'I'm sure he'll make an exception in this case.'

There was a pause. 'Can I tell him who's calling, please.'

'A friend.'

Another pause. 'Just that. A friend?'

'Just that.'

A third pause. 'I'll see what I can do.' And the telephone was put down on something hard.

A minute passed, then another, before the receiver was picked up with a rough, 'This had better be fuckin' good, *friend*. Do you know what time it is?'

'Precisely to the minute, Angel,' said Valin in clipped tones. 'Do you?'

'*Colonel*. What the hell! Man, it's great to hear your voice. Wait a minute. I got to get some juice.'

Down went the phone again, Valin heard voices in the background, and Angel came back on the line. 'Sorry, sir,' he said. 'Got to get my domestic arrangements fixed better.'

'How are you, Angel?' asked Valin.

'Great. I went and saw Spense a while ago. I

14

envy him with Carmen. Why can't I find a woman like that?'

'Could your lifestyle have something to do with it, do you think?'

'Could be, Colonel, could be.'

'I just spoke to him.'

'Spense? How the hell is he?'

'Good. He mentioned that he'd seen you.'

'We sure tied one on.'

'Good.' Valin's voice became serious. 'Now, Angel.'

'Sir.'

'The last time we met, you asked me about the possibility of another mission. I have one, and I wonder if you're interested.'

'Where?'

'Scotland.'

'Are you serious?'

'Never more so. There's a little island just off the coast. We have to go in and rescue a damsel in distress.'

'What's the weather like over there?'

'Vile. And getting worse.'

'And the pay?'

'The fee is a million in sterling. We split it equally.'

'How many of us?'

'Maybe ten. Maybe more.'

'Jeez, Colonel, I could make that in a day doing what I'm doing now.'

'Something slightly illegal, I imagine.'

'Could be. But I don't like to talk about it on an open line.'

'Of course you don't.'

'And the weather's great over here.'

'I imagine it would be.'

'And the women . . .' He didn't bother to go into details.

'You don't have to spell it out.'

'And I've got a great little place just outside Beverly Hills.'

'And a Mercedes, no doubt.'

'Two.'

'So you're not interested.'

'Shit, Colonel, course I am. I've never been so bored in all my life. When do you need me?'

'Now.'

'I'll be on the first plane. Is Spense coming?'

'Yes.'

'Great. And O'Rourke?'

'He just left Norfolk to join me here in London.'

'The old team.'

'As many of us as are left. There'll be a ticket to London at Tower Travel on Rodeo Drive for you first thing tomorrow.'

'Either Mark or I will be there.'

'Excellent, Colonel. See you soon.'

'See you, Angel,' said Valin, and put down the phone with a smile.

O'Rourke arrived at supper-time. He and Valin ate a scratch meal in the tiny kitchen of the flat, then took glasses of beer into the living-room, where Valin showed the younger man the intelligence that Bryant-Marshall had supplied, and explained the details of the mission.

'Seems pretty straightforward, sir,' said O'Rourke. 'But it looks like this Robertson character's got a good team defending.

'The best. Roland Stone doesn't fool around.'

'You know him, don't you?'

'Yes. We were quite good friends for a while back in the early seventies. But I haven't seen him for years. I had no idea he was even in this part of the world.'

'And Angel and Spenser are in?'

'Yes.'

'So we need a few more hands.'

'Five or six at least.'

'We'd better start recruiting then. Fancy a drink tonight?'

Valin nodded, they both wrapped up warmly,

went out to the Range Rover that O'Rourke had driven down in, and he turned it in the direction of Camden Town, where there was a certain pub that was a meeting-place and recruiting centre for mercenaries.

When they arrived it was quiet, and the landlord, an ex-marine, welcomed them warmly.

'Anyone interesting been in?' asked Valin.

'It's been very quiet, sir,' said the landlord.

'No one we know looking for work?'

'The weather's kept them inside. Or else they're all off to sunnier climes.'

'How about you, Tom? Fancy a nice little earner?' asked O'Rourke.

'I'm too old for that lark, sir. Besides, I fancy my skin too much these days.'

'A pity,' said Valin. 'We could have used a man of your calibre.'

'I'll ask around, sir. It'll get busier later. Are you going to stay?'

'For a while.'

The two men took their drinks to a table in the corner, and sat watching the door. After about half an hour, a thin, weather-beaten individual with long, dark hair came in and ordered a drink. They saw Tom speak to him, and the man studied them in the mirror behind the bar before coming over.

'I believe you're looking for men,' he said. He had an Australian accent.

'That's right,' said O'Rourke.

18

'May I sit down?'

Valin nodded, and the man pulled up a chair.

'My name is Phillips,' he said, 'John Phillips. Out of Perth. I'm looking for a gig.'

'Experience?' asked Valin.

'Australian army. Short-termer. Missed 'Nam. Honourably discharged, but couldn't settle. I got a job with the Sydney police. I killed a man. It was no accident, but they couldn't prove it. They kicked me out, and I drifted round the world. I fought in Africa. Killing gets into the blood. I can handle most weapons. Rifles, semi-autos, machine-guns.'

'Who did you serve under?'

'You name them. And I know you, Colonel. You've got a good rep. I'm broke. Give me a chance – I won't let you down.'

'You don't even know what the job is.'

He shrugged. 'What the hell? It's bound to involve violence.'

'Probably.'

'That's what I do best.'

'Have you got a number?'

'I'm staying at a boarding house in King's Cross.' He reached into his pocket, found some paper and a pen, and scribbled down ten digits. 'I'm there pretty much all day. Then in here at night. The landlady's a decent soul. She'll take a message.'

'OK, John,' said Valin. 'We'll be in touch. But I warn you, we go soon. You'll need to be ready at a moment's notice. I don't think we'll have much time for training and assessment.'

'Suits me,' said Phillips. 'What's the pay like?'

'Very good. A percentage of a million pounds. An equal percentage, depending on how many of us go. A dozen tops, I'd say.'

'Are you serious?'

'Never more so.'

'Jesus, Colonel. I could sure use that sort of money.'

'Couldn't we all?' said O'Rourke. 'But we'll need some sort of references.'

Phillips looked at the pair of them, then undid the buttons on the denim shirt he wore beneath his leather jacket. Underneath it was a T-shirt. He pulled it up to show the dimpled scars of three bullet wounds in his chest. 'Angola,' he said. 'In the late seventies. Nearly didn't get out. And before you say you want to see the guy who did it to me: I killed him. With my bare hands. My commanding officer there was a guy called Stannard. Captain Walter Stannard. He's dead now. But he was a good man.'

'I knew him,' said Valin. 'What was the name of his top sergeant again?'

'Is this Trivial Pursuit, Colonel?'

Valin didn't reply.

Phillips pulled a face. 'His name was Monk. Jack Monk. Ex-Paras. He's dead too. Killed in Cambodia sometime in eighty-four or five.'

'Good enough,' said Valin 'You can get dressed now.'

Phillips adjusted his clothes.

'OK, John,' said Valin. 'You'll do. If the job's a goer, which I think it will be, I'll call you tomorrow afternoon. Otherwise, we'll bear you in mind when one does come up.'

'I'm grateful, Colonel. Just one thing. If it does happen, can I get a sub? I owe a few quid here and there, and don't believe in leaving debts behind me.'

'Don't worry. I don't move without paying something up front. You'll be well looked after.'

'And weapons?'

'It'll all be sorted.'

'Good. I'll be waiting for your call.'

'Whatever happens, I'll be in touch,' said Valin, and Phillips toasted him and O'Rourke, got up and went back to the bar.

'Seems all right,' said O'Rourke, when Phillips was out of earshot.

'Looks good. Let's hope there's a few more like him around.'

But no one showed by the time Valin and O'Rourke had finished a second round, and the two went up to the bar and spoke to Tom.

'Hope you didn't mind me sending Johnny over,' he said. 'But he needs some work.'

'Not at all,' said Valin. 'He seems like a good hand.'

21

'No one else in tonight, I'm afraid,' said Tom. 'I told you it was quiet.'

'Keep an eye out for us, will you,' said Valin. 'You know we'll see you all right.'

'That was never a worry, Colonel,' replied Tom. 'I'll see what I can do. There might be a couple of lads in later for some afters.'

'Some things never change,' said O'Rourke.

'It's a living,' said Tom with a smile. 'Give me a call tomorrow, and I'll let you know.'

'Righto,' said Valin, buttoning his coat. 'Take care of yourself, and I'll be in touch.'

'You take care too, Colonel,' said Tom, and with a nod each to Phillips, Valin and O'Rourke went out into the freezing night air, dodging the lances of icy rain as they hurried to their car.

4

The next morning at around ten Valin called Bryant-Marshall on the latter's direct line. 'I've thought about it,' said the Colonel, after he had identified himself. 'We go.'

'Good. I knew you wouldn't let me down, James. When?'

'You tell me.'

'ASAP.'

'Is our transport ready?'

'I've got a Herc on stand-by at Farnborough, and the submarine's waiting at Newburgh, on the east coast of Scotland.'

'That's good. But I'm not up to strength yet. I've got two men coming in today from the States, and I'm busy recruiting. But it's not easy.'

'Time is of the essence, James.'

'I appreciate that.'

'I have weather forecasts for the area for the next week. Conditions are foul up there, and getting worse.'

'That's not the problem. You didn't tell me that Roland Stone was in charge of Robertson's private army. He takes no prisoners. Believe me, I know. To go in short-handed would be worse than not going in at all.'

'I might be able to help you there. I have a couple of bodies hanging round, getting fat at the taxpayers' expense, who might be of some use to you.'

'Do I know them?'

'Doubtful.'

'I'll have to meet them.'

'Of course.'

'When?'

'Tomorrow.'

'Where?'

'Here.'

'At your office?'

'Don't worry, James, it's quite secure.'

'But I thought I was *persona non grata* in Whitehall these days.'

'I think we can make an exception in this case.'

'Good enough. And I'll need a down payment.'

'How much?'

'Fifty per cent. I have some expenses to cover. Cash.'

'I can't see that being a problem. Come in this time tomorrow, and I'll have the money for you, and you can meet my two men.'

'And ordnance?'

'Bring in a list. You'll have everything you need within a few hours.'

'Good.' And with the shortest of farewells they broke the connection.

Next Valin phoned the pub in Camden Town. Tom answered. 'Hello, Tom,' Valin said. 'Any news?'

'I was just about to phone you myself,' said Tom. 'A couple of lads came in last night, late. Ex-marines, like myself. Good boys both. One Scots, one English. They're just back from doing some subcontracting in the Far East, if you get my drift. I told them to call back today at about two. I hope that's convenient.'

'That's fine,' said Valin. 'I'll look in at around the same time. Thanks, Tom. I'll bring a little something for you. I'm obliged.'

'Always happy to help an old comrade,' said Tom, before they both hung up.

Valin's last call was to the number that John Phillips had given him the previous evening. It was answered by a woman, and after a pause Phillips came on the line.

'Valin. Looks like you've got a job,' said the colonel. 'But we've got to move fast.'

'That's not a problem.'

'Meet me at Tom's place around three, and I'll fill you in further.'

'I'll be there.' And for the third time Valin replaced the receiver.

Mark O'Rourke was sitting in an armchair looking down over the rain-swept square and drinking his second cup of breakfast coffee. He was dressed in a plaid shirt, leather waistcoat, jeans and cowboy boots, and as Valin explained what was going on, he constantly pushed the cow-lick of blond hair off his handsome face. 'Looks like you'll have to collect our American visitors on your own,' said Valin. 'Spenser's plane is due in at one, and Angel's at four. OK?'

'No problem,' said the young lieutenant as he put down his cup.

The American Airlines flight out of Kennedy was dead on time, and O'Rourke was waiting in the arrivals lounge in Terminal Four at Heathrow as the first passengers trickled through the gate.

He spotted Spenser, Carmen and Jesús as they came through, pushing their luggage on two trolleys. Spenser's rangy form was dressed in a similar urban cowboy style to O'Rourke's, Carmen wore a slightly crumpled designer two-piece, and Jesús was immaculate in a cashmere overcoat.

O'Rourke embraced all three when they met, and said: 'It's good to see the old gang together again.'

Jesús shook his grey head. 'And talk about old times, and all the fun we had,' he said.

'Sorry, Jesús,' said O'Rourke.

'It's not your fault, Señor Mark. I shouldn't take it out on you. But I still can't forget what happened to my family.'

'We're your family now, Jesús,' said O'Rourke,

and gently touched the older man on his shoulder.

'I know. It could have been much worse.' And he looked at Carmen and Spenser. 'At least I have not lost everything, like some of my friends in the old country did.'

'And you're in London,' said Spenser. 'I told you I'd show you some of the world.'

'But did it have to be such a damned cold part?'

'Don't worry,' said O'Rourke. 'We've got you booked into a nice warm suite at the Inn On The Park. Four-star, with all the trimmings.'

When they had transferred the luggage to the Range Rover and were on the motorway heading towards central London, O'Rourke brought them up to date with what was happening.

'Otherwise the colonel would've been here to meet you too. But we've got to move fast, and he's out seeing a couple of hands,' he said.

'I hope they're good,' said Spenser. 'We don't need any dead wood on this trip by the sound of it.'

At around the same time, Valin was sitting in the saloon bar of Tom's pub in Camden Town, when two weather-beaten men in the remnants of army uniforms came in, spoke to Tom, looked over at the colonel, and walked over to his table.

'Colonel Valin?' said the bigger of the two, in a broad Glasgow accent.

'That's me.'

'Tom said you might have something for us.'

'Perhaps. Would you care for a drink?'

'Thanks. Two pints of bitter,' said the Scot.

They sat down and Valin went to the bar to order, and as Tom was pulling the pints he took time to study the pair. The Scot was around forty, big and broad, with the remains of his thinning hair shaved close to the top of his head. The other was younger and slimmer, with a full head of brown hair and a thick silver chain around his neck.

Valin took the drinks back to the table and sat down again.

'Cheers,' said the Scot. 'My name's Maddox. Tony Maddox. This is Jackie Bryant.'

The younger man nodded as he sipped at his beer.

'Tell me about yourselves,' said Valin.

Obviously the spokesman for the duo, Maddox said: 'We met in the Marines. I was a corporal, Jackie here a private. We both signed on for the duration. We thought it was a long-term career, but it wasn't. We were given the golden bullet ... What? Three years ago, Jackie?'

Bryant nodded again, but said not a word.

'So we decided to see the world. We were both single with no responsibilities. Europe, Australia, America. That was where the money ran out. So we hired ourselves out freelance. We've been everywhere: Bolivia, Belize, Iraq, Iran, Bosnia, Rwanda.

You name it. Then we ended up in China with some warlord or other. I've got some photos.' Maddox reached inside his combat jacket and brought out a folder. Inside were dozens of photographs of him and Bryant in various countries with various mercenaries, some familiar to Valin, some not. 'But it's getting more difficult,' Maddox went on. 'The fucking UN gets in everywhere these days.'

'Not where we're going,' said Valin.

'Then Tom told us about you looking for men. You've got a good rep, Colonel. You treat people fair.'

'I'm flattered.'

Then Bryant broke his silence. 'We've fought with you before,' he said.

Valin looked at him and cocked his head, a puzzled expression on his face. 'Where?'

'Goose Green. We followed you through. The SAS glory boys. You do remember that one, don't you?'

'I remember it.'

'Good. Well, that was us. The ones that came behind, clearing up your mess.'

'Is that right?'

'Sure. You looked like you needed someone to watch your back then, and it looks like you need someone to watch your back now.'

'Do I?'

'Obviously. A bit short-handed, are you? Desperate, like? Clutching at straws? Scraping the barrel?'

'Jackie. Leave it,' said Maddox, making an apologetic face at Valin.

Valin ignored the Scot. 'You could say that,' he said. 'And you could be right.'

'So what's the job, Colonel?' asked Bryant. 'If you don't mind me asking, like.'

'I don't mind.' And Valin explained the bare bones of the mission, revealing as few details as possible.

When he told them about the pay, Maddox said: 'We could retire on that.'

'Maybe,' replied Valin, as he spotted Phillips come into the pub, look round, spot the trio, then go to the bar and order a drink. 'But you'd have to come out alive first. How do I get in touch?'

'You can leave a message here,' said Maddox. 'We're kind of moving around at the moment.'

Sleeping rough, thought Valin, but said nothing. 'Fair enough. But keep in contact with Tom. When we go, we go fast. Now I've got someone else to talk to. Nice meeting you.'

'That's mutual, Colonel,' said Maddox. Bryant said nothing, just lit a cheap cigarette and sipped some more beer as if it had to last.

Valin got up and took himself and his drink to where Phillips was perched on a bar stool.

'Colonel,' said the Australian. 'How's it going?'

'Could be worse. Know those two I was talking to?'

'They've been hanging round for a couple of

weeks. The big fella's all right, but I could do without the other one.'

'Too right.'

Valin called Tom over to refill their glasses, and voiced his doubts. 'They come as a package,' said Tom as he put their drinks in front of them. 'That's the way they work. But don't be too hard on Jackie. They've had it rough over the past few months. He's getting edgy.'

'Fine,' said Valin, when Tom had left him and Phillips alone, and Valin had brought the Australian up to speed on developments. 'Another balls-up. I'm supposed to go with two men I've never met. One I could happily live without, but I have to have as part of a package deal, in terrible weather, against fifty men led by a firecracker, and all on the hurry-up without any chance of working out our strengths and weaknesses before we go.'

'Sounds about par for the course then, Colonel,' said Phillips.

'Doesn't it just,' replied Valin with a wry smile. 'Are you sure you want to go?'

'Just try and stop me.'

'Good man. I knew you were sound,' said Valin, and he took one of his cards out of his wallet and gave it to the Australian. 'This is my London address and number. But for now we've got adjacent suites at the Inn On The Park, where my US troops are billeted. One-double-o-seven and eight. We'll be using one as a temporary

HQ until we go. Be there tomorrow at five for a full briefing, OK?'

'Absolutely, Colonel. And some wages?'

'Certainly. We must never forget the wages, must we?'

Angel's plane was delayed by about fifteen minutes, but he was the first at the terminal gate, carrying just a cabin-luggage bag. He was tanned and fit-looking, although his eyes were bloodshot. He saw Mark O'Rourke straight away, grinned and gave him a wave. When he joined him they stood and looked at each other. O'Rourke was still in cowboy mode, and Angel wore a white silk suit that was rather the worse for wear after his journey.

'You'll freeze,' said O'Rourke.

'We don't have a lot of call for overcoats where I've been living.'

'How are you?'

'All the better for seeing you, buddy,' said Angel, and they embraced like the old friends they'd become.

'Come on,' said O'Rourke. 'The car's outside.'

They went out to the car park, and almost immediately Angel started to shiver in the freezing wind. 'Jesus,' he said. 'What have I let myself in for this time?'

'It'll be even colder where we're going,' said O'Rourke. 'First thing tomorrow we go and get you some cold-weather gear.'

They were back at the hotel by five-thirty, where Valin was waiting with Spenser, Carmen and Jesús. Valin had made a detour in the cab on the way back from Camden Town to collect from Eaton Square the intelligence that Bryant-Marshall had supplied, and it was now spilled over the dining-table in the sitting-room of Spenser and company's suite.

When everyone had greeted everyone else, and they had all had a drink, he filled them in on all the latest information.

'Christ,' said Angel. 'You're going to hire a couple of hobos, and take another pair of guys that this Bryant-Marshall pulls out of his hat. I mean, Colonel, didn't it occur to you for a minute that they might run back to teacher carrying tales.'

'I don't give a damn what they do,' said Valin. 'As long as they can shoot straight. We don't have to marry them. Right now we can use all the men we can get. Anyway let's meet them before we pronounce sentence.'

'OK, Colonel,' said Angel. 'You're the boss.'

'Right,' said Valin, then got up and went over to the table. 'This is it, lady and gentlemen,' he said, tapping the pile of paper and photographs. 'The island of Lochnercrag. About as unfriendly and impenetrable as it could be. Except by the front door, which is covered by the guns in this fortress.' He picked up the photo of the harbour, tapped the likeness of the blockhouse and let the thin card float to the floor. 'Not an attractive thought. Especially as Major Roland Stone is sitting pretty on it, with fifty of what are undoubtedly hand-picked and highly trained men. Our only advantage is surprise. We need to get in, take control of the island, free the girl and get out before they know what's hit them.'

'Sounds like it might be easier said than done,' said Spenser laconically.

'Ever the doubting Thomas, Chris,' said Valin. 'I swear you'll never change.'

Spenser shrugged.

'So there it is,' said Valin. 'Right now you know as much as me. Tomorrow we'll know more. So what I suggest is that we go down and have dinner. I believe the chef here is quite good.'

'Sure,' said Angel. 'But let's try his cooking before we pronounce sentence.'

5

They all met for breakfast early the next morning in Spenser's suite, and the dishes were cleared by eight-thirty.

'Here's the plan for the day,' said Valin. 'At ten I present myself at Bryant-Marshall's office in Whitehall. There I will collect half a million in cash, meet our prospective recruits, and be brought up to date on what is happening on Lochnercrag. Then I'll return here. Chris, I want you to come with me. Half a mill is a lot of money, and I don't relish the thought of being deprived of it by some chancer. I want you to carry this.' He picked up the briefcase he had brought with him, put it on his knee and opened it. Inside was a shoulder holster containing a .38 Colt Detective Special revolver. 'I know it's just a popgun to you, but I'll feel better if I know you've got it.' He pulled open the jacket of his suit to show a similar weapon nestling in oiled leather, under his armpit.

'Meanwhile, Mark, you go off with Angel and pick up some cold-weather gear. Everything. Thermals, boots. The lot. You'd better go too, Carmen.

You know Chris's sizes. Pick up enough for all of us. Any late-comers can be accommodated in due course. Use the Amex, Mark. We'll replenish it with cash later. This afternoon at five we have a full briefing here, when the rest of you can meet John Phillips, an Australian that Mark and I met the other day. He seems more than competent. I'm still worried about our numbers, but we'll have to live with that for now. And finally, ordnance. I prepared a list.' He took a sheet of paper from his briefcase and placed it on the table. 'If you'd all care to check that, I'd be grateful for any further suggestions.'

The list was simple. It read:

One Gatling 7.62 M134, adapted for hand use, plus five thousand rounds; five 9mm Uzi machine-pistols plus magazines and five thousand rounds; five V261 7.62 Scorpion machine-guns plus silencers, magazines and five thousand rounds; ten Browning High Power handguns plus magazines, holsters and five thousand rounds; five Colt .45 1911A handguns plus magazines, holsters and twenty-five hundred rounds; five Remington 12-gauge pump-action shotguns plus one thousand cartridges; one dozen Randall No. 1 knives; HE, smoke and flash grenades.

'Planning on starting a war, Colonel?' asked Angel.

'Only a small one. Anything else we need?'
They all agreed that the list was complete.
'Very well, then. Shall we prepare ourselves?'

Valin and Spenser arrived just before ten at the
venerable old building in Whitehall that housed
Bryant-Marshall's office. The weather outside was
getting worse, with snow flurries interspersed amid
the cold rain, and the wind gusting almost to gale
force. They were led by a uniformed sergeant down
long, quiet corridors to an ante-room, where they
waited for five minutes before Bryant-Marshall
himself collected them.

'Sorry to keep you waiting,' he said, after Valin
had introduced Spenser. 'Please come on through.'
He took them back across the corridor to his comfortable office overlooking Horse Guards Parade,
where two other men were sitting in armchairs in
front of an open fire.

'Homely,' said Spenser.

'It's a perk,' replied Bryant-Marshall, and introduced the two strangers. 'Toby Willis,' he said as
a young, fit-looking man sprang to his feet, hand
outstretched. Both Spenser and Valin took it. 'And
Jason McCall.' The other man was slightly older,
with thinning hair and suspicious eyes. He didn't
offer his hand, and Valin looked at Spenser.

'Toby is a captain in Special Ops, Jason a sergeant
in supply,' said Bryant-Marshall. 'At least they're
supposed to be. They're sort of floating about at

the moment, looking after me. I thought they might come in useful. Coffee anyone?' He got on the phone and ordered a pot for five.

'It must be nice to have such an abundance of riches,' said Valin. 'And talking of riches . . .' He didn't finish the sentence.

'Of course,' said Bryant-Marshall. Your filthy lucre. I have it here.' And he went to a filing cabinet, unlocked it, and pulled out two briefcases. 'Do you want to count it?'

'I trust you,' said Valin.

'That's reassuring,' replied Bryant-Marshall. 'You'll receive the balance on the completion of the mission. Now what about these two reprobates?' He indicated Willis and McCall. 'They're fully up to the job. Trained to the hilt. I can assure you of that.'

'And I presume they won't want payment,' said Spenser, speaking for the first time. 'Already being on your payroll and all.'

'I never thought of that,' said Bryant-Marshall. 'What do you say, men?'

Neither of the two replied, and the conversation was interrupted by a middle-aged woman coming in, wheeling a trolley that contained coffee and biscuits.

When the coffee was poured, Bryant-Marshall said to Valin: 'Well?'

'I prefer to choose my own troops,' said Valin.

'I'm afraid circumstances preclude that at the

38

moment,' said Bryant-Marshall. 'The weather's come down in the operational area, and it bodes even worse. The worst in living memory, so they say. Even the submarine commander is getting worried. And we've got to land a plane there. It looks like you go within thirty-six hours, or you don't go at all.'

'Jesus,' said Valin, looking at Spenser. 'There's only five of us at the moment.'

'Then take my boys. That'll being you up to seven.'

'And those other two guys,' said Spenser. 'Couldn't we use them?'

'That's still only nine,' replied Valin. 'Oh, very well. You two,' he said to Willis and McCall. 'I don't care what the hell you are here. When you're with me, you're both privates. You take orders from the people I designate. And when they say jump, you say, "How high and how often?" Understood?'

The two men nodded, but not happily.

'Right. Be at the Inn On The Park at five this afternoon for a briefing. Suite one-double-o-seven. And get kitted out for the weather. You can go now. I want to speak to Hadley. Spenser, You stay.'

Willis and McCall left without a word.

'This is a fucking shambles, Hadley,' said Valin, when they'd gone. 'But we'll make what we can of it. I have here . . .' – he took his list of weapons from his inside pocket – 'the ordnance I need for the mission. How soon can I have it?'

Bryant-Marshall took the paper and scanned it. 'Heavy-duty,' he said. 'This evening. There's a place in Croydon we use. Toby will take you there after the briefing. Is that all right?'

'Fine,' said Valin. 'Transport?'

'It'll be supplied. And I'll lay on a bus to take you down to Farnborough tomorrow. You'll need to be away by noon.'

'Christ,' said Valin. 'Fred Fucking Karno's army.'

When Valin and Spenser got back to the hotel, the suite was strewn with new cold-weather clothing of every description. 'You've got enough for us twice over,' remarked the colonel. 'Good. It looks like we're going to need it. We go tomorrow at noon. Now where have you hidden the bloody phone?'

It eventually turned up under a pile of thick woollen sweaters, and Valin phoned Tom. 'Have Maddox and Bryant been in?' he asked.

'They're here now.'

'Let me speak to Maddox.'

There was a pause, and Valin could hear an old Beatles tune in the background, then Maddox's Glasgow accent.

'Colonel,' Maddox said.

'You're hired,' said Valin. 'There's a briefing tonight at five.' He told Maddox where. 'I'm going to send my aide round now with some money. I want you to get some decent clothes. Otherwise the management here will have

40

you slung out. And get a good meal. And stay sober.'

'Of course, sir.' Maddox sounded offended. 'We're professionals.'

'And try and get your oppo to get his mind right. This is going to be a difficult enough mission as it is. I don't need anyone with an attitude problem. Can you handle that?'

'Sir.'

'Good. As from now, you're back in the service. Don't forget that.' He put down the phone and turned to O'Rourke. 'Mark, take a thousand pounds in cash round to Tom's. Find Maddox and Bryant. Tom'll point them out to you. Give them the cash. If they run out on us, so be it. It's better now than later. And very little financial loss. If they turn up, then they come with us.'

'Sir,' said O'Rourke briskly.

6

Everyone was on time for the briefing, everyone was sober, and everyone had come. This is a motley bunch, Valin thought, as he looked round the sitting-room of the suite, where every seat was full. But what the hell can I do about it?

He introduced everyone by name, and designated O'Rourke as second in command, and Angel as sergeant, much to his and Spenser's amusement. 'These are my right and left hand,' said Valin. 'When they speak, they speak for me. Anyone who disagrees with that should leave now.'

There were no takers.

From somewhere O'Rourke had foraged a room divider upholstered in hessian, and to it he'd pinned the map and photographs of Lochnercrag, and Robertson, Roland Stone and Vanessa Petersham. 'Some of you know where we're going, and why,' said Valin. 'Some of you don't. Bear with me if you've heard all this before.' Then he explained the mission fully for the last time.

When he was finished, he said: 'Does anyone have any problems so far?'

Once again there were no takers.

He repeated the list of weapons he'd requisitioned, and said: 'I assume there's something there for everyone. I apologize for not knowing all your specialities, but this mission was accepted at very short notice.'

No one volunteered a comment.

'Right. Any questions?'

Carmen spoke up. 'Who's feeding the Gatling?'

'I don't know. Chris?' said Valin.

'Dunno, sir.'

'I'll do it, then,' said Carmen. 'You need an expert for the job.'

'You want to come?' Valin was surprised.

The girl's dark eyes flashed. 'Did you think I was here for a winter vacation, Colonel?' she snapped.

Valin smiled. 'Did you know about this, Chris?' he asked.

Spenser shrugged.

'What's it like being pussy-whipped, son?' asked Angel with a grin.

'Piss off,' said Spenser.

'Calm down, boys,' said Valin. 'Carmen proved her worth on our last mission. And if she wishes to accompany us again, then I for one have no objections. Does anyone else?'

There were no comments from the floor.

'Good. Then you're in, Carmen.'

The young woman smiled, and squeezed her husband's hand.

'Tonight we go and inspect the weapons and ammunition,' said Valin. 'Toby, what's the drill?'

'They're waiting in Croydon for us now. We'll go and check them out when we finish here. Then they'll be driven down to Farnborough, and kept under guard until tomorrow when we collect them, before we're flown to Scotland.'

'So there are some advantages to being on the side of right,' said Valin drily. 'Chris. You, Angel and Maddox will accompany Toby and myself to inspect our cache of goodies. Meanwhile I've booked Maddox and Bryant into a slightly less salubrious establishment than this one, in Victoria, for the night with John here. I suggest that you all collect your stuff and get a good night's rest. I have the latest weather forecasts from the area of Lochnercrag. It's abysmal up there. Twenty-foot seas, hurricane-force winds, snow and sleet. Even the submarine commander is wetting himself about the trip. And believe me, when submarine commanders do things like that, the conditions are Bad with a capital B. I just hope our plane can land OK. At least no one on the island will be expecting us, which is an advantage. And believe me, we need all the advantages we can get right now. Before we go, Phillips, Maddox and Bryant should check out the surplus cold-weather gear that's in the other room. There's enough to kit out an army, even if we don't have one. If you're short of anything, you still have tomorrow morning to get what you need.

And finally, I have made up some wage packets. You all know the deal. Fair shares all round. But I took the liberty of banking the cash I received this morning. Don't worry, the bank manager has my instructions in case I don't make it back. But as we have such a short time before we go, and some of you are only in temporary accommodation, I felt it too risky to leave large sums of cash lying around. I've kept back ten thousand in cash for each of you, Willis and McCall included, although what Bryant-Marshall will say I don't know. I hope no one has any objections. Jesús here, who will not be accompanying us on this trip, is authorized to collect the surplus after the mission if, for any reason, I can't. Mark is also a co-signatory. Just look after the boy, and you'll all be fine.'

There were no objections again, and with that the meeting broke up and everyone went about their various tasks.

At seven o'clock Valin, Maddox, Spenser, Willis and O'Rourke were in the Range Rover, heading south out of London through the thinning rush-hour traffic. O'Rourke was driving. The weather was fiendish, and even in the suburban streets the wind was strong enough to rattle the sides of the heavy, four-wheel-drive vehicle.

'Just wait till we get to Scotland,' said Maddox as they rumbled towards Croydon, 'if you think this is bad.'

'At least you'll be at home,' said Spenser.

'I have no home now,' replied Maddox. 'The British army was my home.'

'I'll say amen to that,' said Valin from the front of the car. 'And there's an awful lot more of us out there would agree.'

'And it's getting no better,' said Willis. 'I've had three regiments disbanded on me in the last five years.'

'Bloody politicians,' grumbled Maddox. 'They have no idea of what that means to a man.'

'Well, at last we're being paid properly to help

them out this time,' said O'Rourke.

'True,' agreed Valin. 'In times of trouble, they always turn to people like us.'

The warehouse where the guns were being stored was in a dark backstreet to the east of Croydon, and Willis directed O'Rourke through a maze of badly lit turnings until they got there. Then he jumped out of the Range Rover into the driving rain, and knocked on an anonymous metal door daubed with graffiti.

It was opened in a second, and Willis showed his ID, then beckoned for the others to join him. They went into a dim cavern of a building where three heavily armed military policemen were guarding an articulated lorry with a huge wagon hitched to its tractor.

'Open her up,' said Willis to the sergeant who was in command of the guards. The man did as he was told, and hauled open the huge rear door of the wagon. Inside was a pile of smaller boxes, and Willis clambered in, found a light and switched it on. The other four joined him, and they started to lever the top off the boxes. Inside, neatly stored in oiled wrappings, were the weapons that Valin had requisitioned.

Spenser found his Gatling right away, hauled it out of its box and quickly checked it. 'Pretty good,' he said as he put it back, and inspected the belts of cartridges that had been supplied. 'These'll do. What else have we got?'

Valin was pleased to see that everything he'd asked for was there, and said to Willis: 'Good work at such short notice.'

'Sir Hadley has ways and means. Are you satisfied, sir?'

'Absolutely.'

'Shall we get back to town, then? I have a few last-minute things I need to do.'

'Of course. And this will all be waiting for us tomorrow?'

'All present and correct, sir,' said Willis, as he stood to attention and threw the colonel a parade-ground salute.

8

D-Day started early, with everyone meeting again in Spenser's suite. This time they were all togged up in their cold-weather gear, and Valin wondered what the management of the hotel would think as they all trooped out, leaving just Jesús to stay in solitary splendour in two of their high-priced suites. Fuck them, he thought, if they can't take a joke.

As promised, a luxury coach with darkened windows was waiting at the back of the hotel at noon to take the troops down to Farnborough. 'War games,' said Angel to a surprised receptionist as the ten-strong raiding party walked through reception and out into the fierce rain and wind that struck across Hyde Park.

They were in Farnborough within two hours, and the Hercules C-130 transporter, adapted for passenger use, and already loaded with the weapons and ammunition, stood on the runway, huge and black, with just a single RAF roundel on each side of its fuselage and the top and bottom of its wings, for identification.

The pilot introduced himself and his crew, but it

was obvious that he didn't approve of the bunch of men who took their places on the thinly upholstered seats that ran up both sides of the cabin.

When they were airborne and well on the way, the pilot came back into the body of the Hercules for a talk with Valin. 'It's going to be a hairy landing,' he said above the din of the engines. 'Most other planes are grounded in the sector where we're heading. The weather's hell up there.'

'We'll survive,' replied Valin. 'We've all seen worse.'

'I hope so,' said the pilot. 'There's sick-bags in the back of the seats, just in case.'

It was indeed a hairy landing at the naval base near Newburgh, with a ferocious gale blowing thick snow across the runway, almost obscuring the landing lights that were necessary in the darkness of the Scottish night that fell so early at that time of year. There were more than one or two sets of white knuckles before the plane taxied close to the control tower.

The nine men and one woman evacuated the aircraft quickly, and ran through the blizzard to the tower, leaving half a dozen naval personnel to unload the weapons from the hold of the plane. Once inside Valin was immediately buttonholed by a young lieutenant, who introduced himself as the executive officer of Her Majesty's Submarine *Exodus*.

'An apt name,' said Valin, shaking snow off his forage cap. 'What's the drill, Lieutenant?'

'You stay here tonight. The sub is moored at a harbour about five miles down the road. My commander won't move in the dark. We leave at first light, which won't be until about ten, if the last few days are anything to go by. It won't be a long journey. You should be at the island within an hour or so. Your equipment is being loaded into a lorry as we speak. We have four cars to take you and your men . . .' He stopped and cleared his throat as he saw Carmen shuck off her padded jacket. 'Your people,' he corrected himself. 'I'll be staying here with you. The canteen has hot food, and the bar will be open afterwards. For obvious reasons we're keeping you separate from the base personnel. As far as they're concerned you're Special Forces on a training mission. Please don't make it too obvious that you aren't. If you'll follow me I'll show you to your quarters.'

Valin and the team followed the lieutenant through to a barracks on the far side of the building. The colonel was given a room of his own, as were Spenser and Carmen when their relationship was explained. The other seven were split into three rooms. Maddox and Bryant in one, Willis and McCall in another, Angel, O'Rourke and Phillips in a third. When they had stowed away the little gear they had brought with them, the lieutenant led them back to the canteen, empty except for three women, who served them their supper.

After the meal, they all gathered for a drink in the bar. But with the prospect of what was to come, it was a very subdued party, and within a few hours everyone decided to call it a day, and headed off to bed.

The next morning the team was called for breakfast at seven, which was served by the same three women in the same empty canteen. Outside, wet snow beat against the windows strengthened by chicken wire, from a sky so black it seemed impossible that daylight would ever come again, and the temperature was well below zero, with a wind chill that brought it down even further.

The lieutenant joined them for their eggs, sausage, baked beans, bacon, toast, and a choice of tea or coffee, and sat with Valin and O'Rourke.

'It's bloody rough out there,' he said. 'Getting on to that island is going to be no joke.'

'That's our job,' said Valin.

'And unfortunately it's ours to help you,' said the naval officer stiffly.

'Relax, Lieutenant,' said the colonel. 'I know how you feel. I was a regular for long enough. We're a bloody nuisance. And doing something you could do much better, left to your own resources. Isn't that right?'

'Something like that, sir.'

'Only your lords and masters have decided that we're the people for the job. I understand that that rankles. But frankly, Lieutenant, that's just too bad. You have your orders, and we have ours. I suggest that we all carry them out like the professionals we are, and don't allow personal feelings to interfere. Is that reasonable?'

'Sir.'

'Good. Now when do we leave for the sub?'

'As soon as you've finished eating.'

Valin placed his knife and fork carefully together on his empty plate. 'Then let's go,' he said.

Four anonymous, dark-blue Ford Granadas, each complete with a driver in civilian clothes, were waiting outside the barracks in the driving snow. The troops, all bundled up in warm clothing, piled into the transport, and with headlights on full beam, they slowly moved out from the base, followed by a five-ton lorry containing the weapons and the lieutenant.

It was a short drive, and it was still dark when the convoy stopped outside a barrier guarded by two naval police in a small hut, overlooking a tiny harbour which was filled to overflowing by the lean, black shape of a submarine. The cars and the lorry were waved through, pulled up at a jetty, and met by two ratings carrying automatic weapons. The squad left the cars, as more ratings were summoned to unload the lorry, and with the lieutenant they scrambled up the gangplank on to the slippery surface of the sub, up into the conning tower, and down into the claustrophobic interior of the vessel.

They were greeted, if that was the word for the terse acknowledgement that he gave, by the commander of the sub. The lieutenant introduced him as Captain Colby, and he led the eleven of them down to the ward-room, which was barely big enough to accommodate them.

'I'll be brief,' he said. 'As soon as your kit's loaded, and it gets light, we'll cast off. I'll submerge outside the harbour and surface to the north of Lochnercrag. The seas are pretty high out there, I warn you. If any of you are prone to seasickness, be prepared to lose your breakfast, and even if you aren't, you probably will anyway.' That at least seemed to give him some modicum of satisfaction. 'Before we go, the lieutenant here will show you the two inflatables we have ready to get you from us to the island. They're pretty flimsy, and I for one wouldn't want to use them in these conditions. But needs must, I suppose.' This too seemed to improve his temper.

So we might all drown, thought Angel, from his perch on the ward-room table. And a jolly good show too, as this fucking Brit would probably put it.

The commander was interrupted by the phone. He picked it up, barked 'right' into the receiver and then replaced it. 'We're loaded and battening down,' he said. 'We'll be off shortly. Lieutenant, you'd better show these ... ah ... gentlemen – and lady too – where their goods and chattels are stowed. I probably won't be seeing them again.' With that, and no words of farewell, he left the room.

'Nice chap,' commented O'Rourke. 'Full of the joys.'

'He'll get you where you want to go. That's the main thing,' said the lieutenant, as the submarine's engines were started, and the hull vibrated to their sound. 'Now if you'll come this way, I'll show you your supplies.'

The boxes of weapons and ammunition had been piled haphazardly in a narrow corridor at the stern of the craft, and immediately the team began to break them open.

Willis and McCall both went for silenced Scorpions and Browning automatics, with spare ammunition magazines in shoulder bags that had been thoughtfully included. Valin chose a Colt .45 and an Uzi. O'Rourke slung a third Scorpion on his shoulder, and also went for the heavy Colt. Angel took both an Uzi and a Scorpion, and selected the US government-issue Colt as a side-arm. Bryant picked one of the Remington pump-action shotguns and an Uzi as backup, and strapped a holstered Browning around his waist. Maddox settled for just a shotgun and a Colt, and Phillips took one of the

Israeli-manufactured 9mm's and a similarly cham-
bered Browning. Spenser and Carmen shared the
Gatling, and both chose Brownings as side-arms.
And they all added one of the heavy, razor-sharp
knives to their personal arsenals, and a selection
of grenades and spare cartridges were distributed
between their pockets and bags. The remaining
weapons were tossed back into the boxes and left
for the cleaners, as Willis put it.

There was a powerful radio rig included. It
was to be used to communicate with the sub,
which would be lying to, submerged, close to
the island, to let the commander know when
the mission was completed, and that the party,
plus Lord Petersham's daughter, were ready to be
collected. It was big and awkward, and Phillips
drew the short straw, and was designated radio
operator.

There were other supplies too, which the powers
that be had decided were necessary for the job:
compasses, first-aid kits, and so on, which all had
to be packed away before the mercenaries were
ready to go.

After much loading and checking of the action of
the various weapons, the team declared themselves
satisfied, and the lieutenant took them to look at the
inflatables that would transfer them to the island.
As he did so, the submarine slowly started to move
away from the harbour and into the rougher, open
seas, where the signal to submerge was given, and

they felt the vessel sink down into the calmer waters beneath the waves.

The inflatables were each capable of carrying six passengers, had large outboard motors fitted at the rear, and were the same deep grey as the sea itself. They were also extremely light and fragile-looking, and each member of the party felt some trepidation at the sight of them.

'Jesus,' said Angel. 'I got stronger-looking boats in my bath.'

'No doubt,' said Valin. 'But these will do the job. And as the man said: if you're a lousy sailor, you're going to lose your breakfast.'

'Fuck,' said Bryant. 'I get seasick on the Serpentine.'

'Then prepare to get *very* sick,' said Valin.

The submarine glided through the dark waters towards the island, and within what seemed a very short time to Carmen and the waiting men, the signal was given to surface. The sea felt very different when they did. Everyone could hear its roar, even through the twin hulls of the sub, and the vessel was tossed about like a leaf.

'Fuck's sake,' said Angel. 'What the hell are we getting into this time?'

'Life-jackets,' said the lieutenant, who showed them a pile of the fluorescent-orange garments. 'And make sure they're done up properly. Your future may depend on it.'

When everyone had put on their Mae Wests, the

lieutenant shrugged into a set of oilskins, and he, plus two similarly attired ratings, with the help of Willis, McCall, Bryant and Maddox, manhandled the inflatables into the conning tower, and one of the ratings opened the largest of the two hatches. All of them were immediately soaked, as water poured in. The sealed bulkheads kept the water from getting into the rest of the sub, but the tower area was soon knee deep with freezing sea water, and with great difficulty the small boats were pushed out on to the greasy skin of the sub. The waves loomed over the boat, and everyone clung for dear life to any protuberance they could find on the hull, as the boats were launched. Over the roar of the sea and the wind, the lieutenant screamed: 'The island's due south, less than a quarter of a mile away.' Nothing was visible through the worsening weather. 'We'll submerge again in three minutes, so be quick. And good luck. You're going to need it,' he added, and without another word he and the ratings went back inside the boat and slammed the hatch behind them.

9

And so started the most terrifying and hazardous journey that any of the participants had ever made. A journey that, although short, seemed endless, and left the group exhausted. And that featured in their nightmares for years to come.

As soon as the hatch on the conning tower clanged shut, Valin jumped into the first boat, took the tiller, and as previously arranged, was joined by Carmen, Spenser, Maddox and Bryant. The other five took the second boat, with O'Rourke at the helm, which was connected to the first with a nylon line, and they started the engines. Luckily, both caught immediately, and they pushed off from the hull of the sub into the full force of the weather, and before it submerged and pulled them down into the depths with it, the two inflatables turned due south towards Lochnercrag, which although it was close, was invisible through the blizzard that blew from Russia.

The wind was coming hard from the east, and Valin's boat immediately began to tip over, and they only regained stability when both Spenser and

Maddox dived across the bottom of the inflatable and managed to stabilize it.

Even though the boats were connected, the waves and spray were so fierce that they lost sight of each other immediately, and the powerful outboards were almost powerless against the strength of the sea.

The wind was relentless, carrying snow and sleet hard against the two small boats, and everyone on board who was not busy steering them in the direction of the island was busy bailing out the water that threatened to sink them.

And then the worst happened. A freak gust caught O'Rourke's boat and spun it round in a semicircle and the line connecting the two tautened and snapped. The last Valin saw of the other boat was a view of the bottom of the craft as a wave lifted it and tossed it away from his, and into the slate-grey daylight, like a child's toy.

'We've lost them,' yelled Spenser, and held up the end of the nylon line. 'Did you see anything?'

'I don't know,' replied Valin at the top of his voice. 'I think they might've capsized.'

'Let's have a look.'

But although they circled slowly, there was no sign of their companions or their small boat.

'We'll have to press on,' said Valin. 'We've got to get to the island.'

This they did, as Bryant, who had abandoned his task of bailing out the inflatable, lay on the bottom of the boat in the freezing water, throwing up the contents of his stomach.

'Look after him,' screamed Valin to Maddox. 'And make sure he doesn't lose his weapons.'

So much for the tough guy with attitude, he thought. I just hope he does a better job in combat.

The boat heaved and yawed as it was taken by the sea and thrown in almost every direction except the one in which Valin was desperately trying to steer it. He opened the throttle of the engine, and putting all his strength into it, managed to turn the boat on to the right course, and as the wind tried to swing the boat to the west, he pushed it south, almost by force of will.

Christ, he thought, as the wind froze his face and hands, and the icy water found any chink in his clothing, I hope to hell that O'Rourke and the rest are OK.

When the line that connected the two boats snapped, and the wind and waves spun the inflatable that O'Rourke was steering in a full circle, it had almost capsized, but luck was on the vessel's side, and after surfing a massive wave it flopped down, right side up. But all was not well. As the flat bottom of the boat hit the solid surface of the sea, McCall, who had been tossed right to the edge of the inflatable, lost his balance. He dropped the Scorpion he was carrying, it bounced on the top side of the boat, and as he scrambled to catch it, he caught his foot in the loose line and fell overboard. Willis made a mad grab for his arm, connected, then lost his grip on the smooth, wet leather of McCall's jacket and the man was gone. 'Man overboard,' screamed Willis as McCall was washed away to vanish in the snowstorm.

O'Rourke immediately spun the boat in a tight circle and sent it towards where McCall had disappeared, but there was no trace of the supply sergeant.

'Keep going. He's wearing a life-jacket,' yelled Willis.

'It's no good,' shouted O'Rourke, after two or three fruitless minutes had passed. 'We'll never find him in this. And he won't last thirty seconds in the water.'

'Keep fucking looking,' yelled Willis again, as he clawed the Browning from its holster and pointed it in O'Rourke's direction.

Angel slammed the barrel of the Uzi he was carrying down on Willis's wrist, and the sound of the bone snapping was audible even above the roar of the wind and sea. The blond-haired man fell to his knees in the bottom of the boat, clutching his arm, and dropping the gun, which Phillips picked up and stuck in the front of his own gun belt.

'Good work, Angel,' shouted O'Rourke. 'Is he all right, Phillips?'

'Apart from a broken wrist, and a ruined ego,

he'll be fine,' replied the Australian, as he pulled a heavy-duty elastic bandage from the small pack of medical supplies that everyone carried. 'I'll have him right as rain in a minute, if you'll just keep this damn boat steady.' Then he looked at Angel through the driving snow. 'But I'd watch your back for the duration, Yank,' he said as he noted the look of hate in Willis's eyes as he lay in the three inches of freezing water in the bottom of the inflatable, shivering from the cold and shock.

O'Rourke kept steering the boat due south, until after what seemed like an age, suddenly he saw through the snow and spray, rearing up above them, the sheer cliffs on the north side of Lochnercrag. By that time he was exhausted from wrestling with the tiller, and frozen right through. 'Land,' he shouted, and drove the inflatable into a slight lee between two huge rocks that sheltered the craft from the worst of the wind and waves.

Angel climbed to his feet and grabbed hold of an outcrop of rock to steady himself, and looked up at the cliff that towered above them. 'We'll never climb this,' he shouted back at O'Rourke. 'Not with him . . .' – he gestured at Willis – 'in his state. We'll have to go round and find the harbour.'

Valin had more luck with his landfall. As the watch on his wrist read eleven hundred hours plus fifty, he too spotted land. When the inflatable climbed one of the huge waves, he saw the entrance to the harbour as it had been represented in the photos he'd seen, what seemed an eternity before, in the warmth of his London flat. It was a different picture now. Gone was the sunlight that had lit the photographs, and there were no cruisers moored by the jetty. Just one, pulled up on a dry dock. However, the dark shape of the blockhouse, with its gun slits being the only break in its concrete walls, still loomed above the water, keeping guard over the storm-tossed harbour.

Valin slapped Spenser on the shoulder and gestured in the direction of the island. 'See it?' he yelled.

'Gotcha, Colonel,' shouted Spenser. 'But can they see us?'

'I hope they won't be looking. Only crazy people would be out in this weather.'

'Amen to that,' replied Spenser, but his words were torn away by the wind.

Valin steered the inflatable on to the rocky beach at the top of the north side of the 'U' made by the harbour, and everyone tumbled out and pulled the boat up on the pebbles, and stashed it away out of sight. Then they ripped off their brightly coloured life-jackets, which would have made them stand out like ducks in a shooting gallery, bundled them into the bottom of the boat, and crawled into what shelter they could find to check their weapons for damage, and to confer.

'What do you think's happened to the others?' asked Carmen.

Valin's face was serious beneath his day's growth of stubble. 'God knows. But we can't afford to wait around and find out. We're all starting to suffer from exposure. We need shelter and a chance to get warm. We're going to have to take the blockhouse. Please God, Mark and the rest have landed somewhere on the island by now. But if the worst comes to the worst and they're lost, we just press on with the job in hand.'

'Jesus, Colonel,' said Bryant, his face pale and his limbs shaking from the effects of his seasickness. 'There's only five of us, and one's a woman.'

'And she's more than a match for you in your present condition, if not always,' said Valin. 'Pull yourself together, man. You're acting like a virgin at an orgy. We took on the job, and we're going to go for it, whatever the odds. Or would you rather try to get back to the mainland in that?' He gestured at the inflatable. 'We wouldn't get five miles. Besides, as we might well have lost our radio, we need to capture a communications centre. Otherwise no one will know what's happening here on the island. *Capisce?*'

'He understands, Colonel,' interrupted Maddox. 'He's just no sailor, that's all.'

'Fine,' said Valin. 'So let's go.'

They made their way along the remains of the beach, then up on to the breakwater, and down behind it again to give themselves cover. And eventually, all soaked to the skin, with icicles beginning to form on their clothes, freezing and stiff, they came out at the back of the blockhouse that covered the harbour.

They kept close to the concrete building, and eventually came to a roadway, upon which was parked a top-of-the-range Suzuki 4×4 jeep with the keys in the ignition, in front of the door to the fortress. Valin tried the door handle. It was locked.

'Shit,' he growled, and pulled Spenser close and whispered in his ear: 'I'm going to knock. Be ready to go in fast. I don't want any warning sent up to the main house. Kill anything that moves.'

He repeated the plan to Maddox and Bryant, and when the Scotsman nodded, Valin banged on the door with his fist.

Nothing happened for a minute, and as Valin prepared to knock again, he sensed rather than heard bolts being thrown on the far side.

He gave a quick thumbs up with his left hand, as the door was thrown open and a bearded face looked through the gap. Valin was holding his Colt .45 in his right hand, and stuck it into the face of the man who had opened the door. 'Not a word,' said Valin to the surprised guard. 'Or I'll kill you.'

The man stepped back, and Valin pushed through the door and looked round. Inside was a hallway leading to a flight of stairs heading upward. No one else was in sight. The man was carrying an M16 rifle in his hand, and wore a holstered pistol on his hip. Valin grabbed the rifle and tossed it back to Maddox. 'On the floor,' he hissed to the guard. 'Face down.'

The man did as he was told, and Valin unholstered the pistol, a Colt Commander Lightweight, and stuck it into the pocket of his jacket. 'How many upstairs?' he hissed.

The man didn't answer right away, and Valin hit him across the side of his face with the barrel of his Colt. 'How many?' he asked again. 'And you'd better tell me the truth, or you're dead.'

'Four,' said the guard.

'What's the set-up?'

'Two above us. One with a radio. The other's cooking lunch.'

Valin almost smiled. 'Cosy,' he said. 'We're just in time, then. I'm sure we could all do with a bite. Other communications?'

'Two telephones through to the main house.'

'Right,' said Valin. 'On your feet and lead the way. But remember, I'll have this gun at your kidneys. One false move and I'll blow them away.'

The man got up as Spenser and Carmen, Bryant and Maddox came through the door and shut it behind them. The silence behind the thick walls of the fortress, after the buffeting they'd taken, was almost uncanny. And immediately they could feel the benefit of the warmth from the central-heating system inside.

The guard, dressed in paramilitary uniform of boots, grey pants and a navy-blue blouson, walked up the stairs in front of Valin.

The steps opened up into a large room with TV monitors along one wall, whose pictures constantly changed as the cameras dotted around the harbour picked up images from outside. Most of the screens showed nothing but the driving snow or the roiling sea, but even so Valin realized that they'd been lucky to get so far without being spotted. Two men were sitting in wheeled office chairs in the room. One was keeping a desultory eye on the monitors, and the other was in front of a powerful radio transceiver. As Valin followed the captured guard into the room, the two men were discussing American football, and he realized that it was as much complacency on behalf of the guards as luck that had got them so far unseen. But then again he thought, not for the first time, that only a bunch of lunatics would be abroad in such conditions.

There were four more M16s leaning up against the wall, and the two men were both wearing holsters similar to the captured guard's, their flaps firmly buttoned down over the butts of their side-arms. To all intents and purposes they were unarmed, and Valin smiled to himself. Roland Stone had to be slipping if this was the way his men behaved.

The individual watching the screens turned as the guard and Valin cleared the last step and said: 'Who the fuck was . . .?' He didn't finish the sentence as Valin pushed the guard into the room and pointed his Colt at the speaker. He put his fingers to his lips as the other men, sensing that something was wrong, turned and saw the five heavily armed mercenaries crowd up the stairs.

He froze as Spenser pushed the barrel of the Gatling at him. 'It'll make a mess of your nice jacket,' he said conversationally. 'Where's the kitchen?'

'Through there and upstairs,' stuttered the radio man as Valin turned down the volume control on his set.

'Maddox, Bryant,' said the colonel. 'Deal, will you. And be careful, there's four rifles in here, and there's only supposed to be three more men. I think our friend here might be guilty of telling porky-pies.'

By the looks in the eyes of the guards, Valin was correct.

'Already noted that, sir,' said Maddox. 'Come on, Jackie.'

Bryant, already seeming much recovered from his ordeal at sea, followed the big Scot quietly through the door in the far side of the room.

'Carmen, guns,' said Valin when they were gone. And Carmen, being careful to keep out of the line of fire, unholstered two more Colt Commanders and put them in the bag she was carrying on one shoulder.

'Any more guns?' said Valin.

'The case there,' said the radio man, indicating a steel box bolted to the wall.

'Keys?' said Valin.

'It's open.'

Valin tugged the door and looked inside the box, where two Winchester Model 1200 repeater shotguns with pistol grips, and a Sterling sub-machine-gun with its magazine in place, were clipped to the back, and on the bottom lay a silenced Beretta 1934 automatic. Valin helped himself to the handgun, checked the magazine was full, and put it in the other pocket of his jacket, then unclipped the carry weapons and stacked them next to the M16s.

They were interrupted as the door opened that Maddox and Bryant had left by.

Spenser's Gatling and Valin's Uzi swung round as one, but they put up their weapons when Maddox stuck his head round the door. And then, when he was sure that the *status quo* had been maintained, he backed in, *his* Uzi trained on the chest of another guard, hands on head. He was followed by yet another soldier, the owner of the spare M16, then Bryant, who had the barrel of his shotgun close to the man in front of him, held with one hand, while in the other he was holding a hot sausage, from which he was taking bites.

'Bingo,' said Valin. 'The missing man.' He turned to the guard that had been captured at the door downstairs and had given them the disinformation about the number of men in the blockhouse. 'You told me lies,' Valin said and calmly took the silenced Beretta from his pocket, racked a round into the chamber and fired twice. The guard was knocked back against the wall, where he stood for a second, a look of amazement on his face, before he slid down the wall, leaving a bloody trail up the white plaster.

'Tie this lot up,' said Valin. 'And Bryant, I don't mind you eating on the job, but you could have brought some for us.'

Bryant grinned for the first time since Valin had met him. 'Plenty more in the pan, Colonel. Enough for everyone.'

Spenser, Maddox and Bryant secured the guards' arms and feet with their own belts and gagged them with strips torn from their uniform shirts, as Valin and Carmen kept guns trained on them.

When they were finished, Spenser said: 'I hope the rest of those sausages haven't burned, Bryant. Come on, let's get some. I'm starving.'

'OK,' said Bryant, and just as they were about to leave the room, Carmen, who was looking at the monitors on the wall, shouted: 'Look!'

All eyes swung in the direction of her pointing finger, and there, at the bottom of one screen, almost invisible through the driving snow, and only really distinguishable by the bright orange of the life-jackets that the occupants were wearing, was the second inflatable, crawling past the breakwater, into the harbour.

'Thank Christ we got here first,' said Valin. 'Chris, Bryant, see if there's enough food for ten.'

10

After grabbing a bite, Valin left and went down to the jetty. He'd almost forgotten how bad the weather was, and nearly lost the door of the blockhouse to the wind as he opened it.

At the sea wall around the harbour he could see nothing when he cupped his eye against the snow and peered through the storm. Then he heard a distinctive click, as the action of an automatic weapon was engaged, and Angel appeared beside him and stuck the snout of a suppressed Scorpion against his ear.

'Hi, Colonel,' said the American. 'I thought it was you, but I didn't want to take any chances. You captured the island singlehandedly, or what?'

Valin pushed the machine-gun's muzzle away from his head, and said: 'Not quite. But just as well we did what we did. We spotted you a mile off. What the hell happened?'

'A lot,' said Angel, and explained quickly.

'So we're down to eight able-bodied men?'

'Always the sentimentalist, eh, Colonel?'

'Where are the rest?'

'Right beneath us.'

Angel leaned over the sea wall and beckoned. The other three appeared directly, Willis leading the way, his arm in a sling. Valin grabbed him right away and dragged him into shelter. 'What the fuck was that all about?' he demanded.

'We could've found him,' said Willis.

'Like hell. If my lieutenant says otherwise, then it's otherwise. I thought you understood that.'

Willis said nothing.

'Come on,' said Valin. 'Let's get in the warm before we discuss this further. You look like death.'

After greeting Phillips, Angel and O'Rourke with a most uncharacteristic hug, Valin led the way back to the blockhouse, where Spenser and Bryant had hijacked the lunch, Maddox was monitoring the radio, and Carmen was keeping an enthusiastic eye on their prisoners.

There was much relief in the greetings, as the two parties met again. The newcomers showed some interest in the smear of blood down the fortress wall, before they dived into the food. But within ten minutes, Valin clapped his hands and said: 'Attention. Mr Willis, I won't mince words, and I'll say this in front of the rest. We're all of equal importance here. You are charged with drawing a pistol on a superior officer. How do you plead?'

'Are you serious?' said Willis.

'Perfectly. This is how we operate here.' He drew his silenced Beretta again, and cocked the hammer.

'You have ten seconds. Plead or die. The choice is yours.'

Willis looked at the gun in amazement.

'What?'

'Five, four . . .' intoned Valin.

'OK, OK,' said Willis. 'I plead guilty.'

Angel stepped forward. 'With extenuating circumstances, sir. He'd just lost his buddy.'

'Silence,' barked Valin. 'Lieutenant O'Rourke?'

'Pretty much as Angel said,' O'Rourke replied. 'Anyone here would've done the same.'

'Very well,' said Valin. 'Are you with us, Willis?'

'Sir.'

'Ready to obey all orders?'

'Sir.'

'Right. The verdict is that you are guilty, but exonerated. And I commiserate about your friend.' He replaced the Beretta. 'Just as well. The sentence is death.' He turned away from the astonished Willis, clapped his hands and shouted: 'Come on, you men. This is just the start. The hard work begins now. Outside. Maddox and Willis, you two stay and keep an eye on this place.'

'What?' said Maddox.

'Just keep monitoring the radio,' said Valin. 'If they spot us, the first thing they'll do is radio down here. When, and if they do, you two come running. Do what you will with the prisoners.'

The four men on the floor writhed as one at his order.

'Otherwise, keep listening on ...' He looked at Phillips and asked: 'What are you transmitting on?'

'Channel ten, sir.'

'Channel ten,' repeated Valin.

'Understood, Colonel,' said Maddox. 'Good luck.'

'We'll take the Suzuki,' said Valin, as the seven troops emerged from the blockhouse, back into the fierce, freezing wind. But as they were about to board the vehicle, Spenser saw headlights coming through the blizzard, followed by the sound of an engine, and an identical car slowly appeared through the snowstorm.

Changing of the guard, he thought, and lifted the Gatling and began to pump high-explosive bullets at the oncoming vehicle.

The others had seen it too, and aimed a hail of shells and shotgun cartridges at the Suzuki, which slewed across the road, and came to a halt with its nose against the sea wall.

The occupants stood no chance, and didn't even have time to return fire before the petrol tank ignited with a whumph, and the vehicle began to burn fiercely.

'Cease fire,' yelled Valin. 'It's done.'

And it was. There was no sign of life from the Suzuki, as the flames melted the snow around it.

'Score two to us, Colonel,' said O'Rourke. 'Do you think anyone else heard the shots?'

'Let's go back inside and see if anything comes through on the radio,' replied Valin.

They all re-entered the blockhouse, where Willis was waiting on the stairs, his Browning in his uninjured hand. 'Christ,' he said, 'we didn't know what was happening.'

'Anything on the air?' asked Valin.

'Check with Maddox,' said Willis. 'But I don't think so.'

And there wasn't. The main house was over a mile away, and the fury of the wind and sea must have swallowed the noise of the shots and the exploding vehicle.

'Not a thing,' said Maddox. 'Let's hope our luck holds.'

'So far so good,' said Valin. 'Five men here, and almost certainly another five in that Suzuki. We've shortened the odds significantly. Now we'd better get out of here, before anyone up at the main house realizes something's wrong.'

They returned to their Suzuki without another glance at the other one, which by now was just a smoking hulk, climbed aboard with Angel at the wheel, who started up, engaged four-wheel drive, did a tight three-point turn, and headed inland.

He switched the lights on to full beam, and slowly drove in the direction of the main house. He peered through the windscreen, as the billows of snow almost obliterated the road, even with the wipers at full speed, and tried to follow the tracks that the other vehicle had left, even though they were rapidly filling in with fresh snow. The last thing he wanted to do was to go off the road, because he feared that even with all-wheel drive he would never get the heavy vehicle back on to the track.

'At least they'll be expecting us,' said Valin. 'Or at least this thing. That'll give us a chance to get close without raising the alarm.'

'And then the shit really hits the fan,' said Angel.

'So what we do is, as soon as we see the entrance to the place, we drop off O'Rourke and Bryant, who can go forward and recce. The plan showed a guard post at the main gate. I'd like that knocked out before we go in. There's forty or so men inside that compound. And I'd like some serious cover. Otherwise we could freeze out here for a week.'

'Understood, Colonel,' said O'Rourke. 'You happy with that, Bryant?'

'Ready and able, Lieutenant,' said the ex-marine. 'Let's give them the shock of their lives.'

'Not so fast,' said Valin. 'Reconnaissance only for the moment. Then come back and let us know what you've seen. Only shoot if you're spotted. Understand?'

'Sir,' said the two men in chorus.

Then, through the flurries of snow, Angel saw storm lights, high on poles. 'Must be the outer perimeter,' he said, as he switched to dipped headlights and brought the Suzuki to a sliding halt.

'Go, go, go,' said Valin, and O'Rourke and Bryant bailed out into the storm and were quickly lost to sight.

They were gone less than three minutes. Suddenly their figures loomed out of the snow again, and they got back into the vehicle.

'Dead right, Colonel,' said O'Rourke, wiping the snowflakes from his hair. 'Two blokes in a gatehouse. We can take it easily.'

'But I want no noise,' said Valin. 'We'll just drive up like we're the guards on relief, and pop them quietly. You two again.'

O'Rourke and Bryant nodded. Angel started the Suzuki, switched the headlights on full beam and let the vehicle drift down the road. The storm lights were almost useless against the weather, but at least they showed the outer limits of the compound, and when he saw the closed barrier and the gatehouse beside it, he slowed even more, and O'Rourke and Bryant eased the back doors open and held them on the latch.

The guards in the gatehouse were obviously more interested in keeping warm than in security, because as the Suzuki got close the barrier lifted.

Angel drove through, then came to a halt once more.

'Now!' barked Valin, and O'Rourke and Bryant bailed out for the second time, and walked, rather than ran, back towards the gatehouse, so as not to alert the two guards inside.

Bryant shoved open the door and O'Rourke stepped in and sprayed the inside of the building with the contents of the magazine of his silenced Scorpion, killing both guards instantly.

'He didn't need me,' said Bryant, when they came back to report that the mission was accomplished.

'I'm glad to see you haven't lost your edge, Mark,' said Valin. 'Right, Angel, let's press on. Time's a-wasting.'

They moved off again. The road wound for several hundred yards before the main house, from where Robertson ruled the island, and the outbuildings, including the barracks, stables and garages, hove into view through the incessant snow.

'We've been lucky so far,' commented Valin. 'We've had it easy. This is where it starts to get difficult. Spenser, Carmen, cover the barracks with the Gatling. Keep the occupants busy. I don't want anyone running around and giving us trouble. Phillips, you stay with them. Use your grenades. Angel, O'Rourke, Bryant, you come with me into the house. God knows who'll be where. We just have to busk it. And for Christ's sake, don't shoot the bloody girl. Or Robertson for that matter. I want a word with him. Everyone else is fair game.'

Everyone in the group acknowledged his orders, and Angel stopped the Suzuki on the snow-covered turning place in front of the imposing doors of Robertson's lair.

'Not the front door. Christ knows how many are waiting behind that. Chris, you'll probably collect fire from in there too. So watch out. Don't expose your flanks.'

'Understood,' said Spenser, as they flung open all four doors of the truck and piled out. Their footsteps muffled by the snow, Valin, O'Rourke, Bryant and Angel ran round the side of the house, where they found a door, which Bryant blew open with three shots from his Remington. Meanwhile Spenser, Carmen and Phillips got behind the body of the Suzuki for cover.

When the blasts from Bryant's shotgun brought faces to the windows of the barracks, Spenser opened fire with the Gatling, spraying the building with fire, imploding windows, and sending the men inside diving for cover.

'They know we're here now,' said Phillips, pulling out the pin from a high-explosive grenade, and lobbing it expertly through one of the broken windows on the ground floor, to explode inside with devastating results. 'The holiday's over.'

Then fire was returned. Not only from the barracks, but from the house itself as Valin had surmised, and to escape the crossfire, the trio huddled behind the back of the Suzuki. Bullets clanged into its body, and they ducked down low. 'Shit,' said Spenser. 'Something tells me they don't like us.'

*   *   *

When the other four burst through the side door, they found a soldier sitting on a chair in the hall, drinking a Coke. It all happened so fast that he barely had time to register the intruders, before Bryant fired his Remington again, and blew a hole in the man's belly, big enough to insert a six-pack. The soldier was knocked off his seat, his gun clattering along the parquet floor, and he died, still clutching his drink, as the quartet rushed past him and deeper into the house.

They saw no one as they clattered down the corridors, but heard the sound of the others' bullets hitting the front of the house. 'Seems like our calling card's arrived,' said Valin as they went.

The place was massive, with high, vaulted halls, their walls hung with swords, pikes and muskets, ancient tapestries and paintings. Along the edges of the main rooms stood gleaming suits of armour and other military relics. Tartan was much in evidence in the furnishings, and the whole house had the air of antiquity about it. Just the place, thought Valin, as they went, for a real laird to live.

Then they met their first resistance. As they moved through the main dining-room, two storeys high, with a minstrel's gallery at one end, a soldier popped up from behind the banister of the gallery and fired a burst from a machine-pistol. The bullets ripped into the highly polished top of the dining-table, and the four mercenaries dived for cover, before returning fire.

Bryant and Valin lay together under the solid-oak table, and O'Rourke and Angel were shielded from the bullets from above by a pair of venerable brown-leather Chesterfields.

Domestic bliss, thought Valin, as he pulled a grenade from his pack, tapped Bryant on the shoulder, and mimed firing a trigger. The younger man nodded his understanding, then as he rolled out from under cover firing, pumping the action of his shotgun as he went, Valin darted from the other side, and hurled the grenade up into the minstrel's gallery. It exploded a split second later, blowing the gallery to matchwood, and mortally injuring the soldier, whom Angel finished off with a burst from his Uzi.

'This place is a fucking maze,' hissed O'Rourke, as the smoke cleared. 'Where the hell is everyone?'

'Upstairs, I reckon,' said Valin. 'In the laird's private quarters.'

'Then let's go upstairs,' said Angel.

'Do we go back or forward?' asked Bryant.

'Forward,' replied Valin. 'The main staircase should be right through those doors.' He gestured at the huge doorway in front of them.

'Come on then, sir,' said Bryant, and he turned the handles and put his shoulders against the doors, which opened as if they were no heavier than feathers.

As he stepped through, he was met by a hail of bullets which cut him down like a felled tree.

And Angel, risking being shot himself, grabbed the Englishman and pulled him back into the dining-room. 'Shit,' he said, feeling for a pulse. 'He's gone.'

'Get back, then,' yelled Valin. 'We'll have to find another way up.'

'What about Bryant?' said O'Rourke.

'Leave him,' said Valin. 'We can't carry the poor bugger with us. Now come on. Let's go.'

At the same time, outside on the turning place where Angel had parked the Suzuki, Spenser, Carmen and Phillips were bearing the brunt of the fire from the majority of the garrison who had been in the barracks and the house when they arrived. Bullets were ricocheting off the metalwork of the Suzuki, all the tyres were flat, and they could smell petrol from the ruptured petrol tank, which was in danger of blowing at any time.

Spenser fired another burst from the Gatling and shouted: 'The house. We've got to get inside. You two make a run for it. I'll give cover. Then cover me.'

'No,' yelled Carmen.

'Go,' screamed Spenser, and as he stood and triggered a longer burst, Phillips grabbed Carmen by her wrist and dragged her towards the open side-door, firing his Uzi as he went, until the magazine was empty.

They got to the corner of the house safely,

Carmen drew her Browning automatic, and when Phillips had reloaded, they laid down a field of fire to allow Spenser himself to make his run.

He did it without incident, and added the last shells from the belt in the Gatling to the barrage, until they all three ran along the side of the house, ducked inside the open door and pushed it shut behind them.

'Close,' said Spenser, as he discarded the empty belt, and Carmen fed in a full one. 'I wonder how the colonel's getting on.'

'Better than this one, I hope,' said Phillips, who had just checked the body of the soldier lying on the floor.

In fact, the colonel wasn't doing too well at all. There seemed to be no staircase leading upwards, in the wing of the house in which he and the other two had found themselves. There were dozens of doors leading into ante-rooms and other corridors, but frustratingly, they couldn't find a staircase.

'This is fucking crazy, Colonel,' said Angel, as they turned another corner, to find themselves at the end of yet another anonymous corridor.

Valin stopped them and studied the plan of the house which he was carrying in his pack. 'We need to find the kitchens,' he said. 'They're at the back. There's two stairways there.'

And then they had a stroke of luck.

Cowering in one of the rooms whose door they

tried, half hidden by an armchair behind which she was kneeling, was a young girl dressed in black, with milk-white skin and long, red hair. She couldn't have been more than seventeen, and when she saw the intruders, she began to cry.

'Who are you?' said Valin, not unkindly.

She didn't answer, but just sobbed all the harder.

'Come on, honey,' said Angel, picking her up from where she was hiding. 'We don't mean you any harm. We're the good guys.'

'You won't hurt me?'

'What? A girl as pretty as you? No, ma'am. We're soldiers of fortune – not murderers.' This wasn't strictly true, given some of their previous adventures, but it succeeded in reassuring the girl somewhat. 'What's your name?' Angel asked.

'Trudy.'

'And what are you doing here?'

'I work here,' she said proudly. 'I'm the new mistress's maid.'

'What, Vanessa Petersham?' Valin butted in.

'That's right.'

'And she's here. In the house?'

'Upstairs.'

'We've come to rescue her.'

'Rescue her,' Trudy echoed. 'Why does she need rescuing?'

'Her father wants her back.'

'Pshaw,' said the girl. 'I don't think she'll welcome the intrusion.'

Valin pulled a face and shrugged at O'Rourke and Angel. 'What do you mean?'

'She seems happy enough here,' replied Trudy.

'That's not what we heard.'

'Maybe you heard wrong.' The young woman seemed to be recovering fast from her fright, and Angel pulled a wry face at O'Rourke.

'Well, whatever,' said Valin. 'We need to find her. Can you show us the way up?'

'I can. But I don't know that I will. Coming in here with guns and all.'

Angel pulled another face, and scarcely suppressed a laugh.

Valin gave him a dirty look. 'Listen, Trudy,' he said. 'I don't propose to discuss the ethics of the matter with you right now. Perhaps another time. But despite what my American friend here said, we don't always behave precisely like gentlemen. So you'd better show us, or else . . .'

'Or else what?' said Trudy bravely.

'Or else I'll never get to see you again,' said Angel, with a rakish smile. 'And that would never do.'

Trudy looked up at the handsome young American, his chin stubbled and his dark hair hanging thickly down over his face. He winked at her, and she said: 'OK, then. They're just down the corridor.'

'Marvellous,' said Valin and shook his head, as Angel peered out of the door through which they'd come. When he saw that the coast was clear, he took Trudy by the hand and led her outside.

'He must have something,' said O'Rourke.

'Certainly,' replied Valin, as they followed Angel and Trudy. 'But I've never been quite able to fathom what.'

As Trudy showed them the direction of the kitchens, they heard the sound of heavy boots on the floor coming their way, and Angel threw Trudy into a doorway and protected her with his body, as Valin and O'Rourke hit the floor, their carry weapons pointing in the direction of the approaching footsteps.

As they cocked their weapons and prepared to fire, Spenser, Carmen and Phillips came barrelling round the corner, and skidded to a halt at the sight of their comrades.

'Don't shoot,' said Spenser laconically. 'We come in peace.'

11

The parties exchanged war stories briefly, and even though they'd hardly known the man, Spenser, Carmen and Phillips were still sick at heart to hear of Bryant's death. 'Two down,' said Spenser. 'That's not good, Colonel.'

'No,' agreed his commanding officer. 'But the other side have paid dearly for both of them.'

'So who's this?' asked Spenser, looking at Trudy.

'Milady's maid,' said Valin. 'She seems to think we've been sold a bum steer,' and paraphrased their conversation about Lady Vanessa.

'Shit,' said Spenser. 'Curiouser and curiouser. So what do we do?'

'Press on, of course. We've got to earn our crust.'

'Right,' said Spenser. 'Let's do it. Any sign of Maddox and Willis by the way?'

'Not so far,' said Valin. 'They must have got a squawk over the air. But it's a long haul by foot from the harbour. Especially in this weather. But I'm expecting them anytime.'

'Good,' said Phillips. 'I was beginning to feel lonely.'

'Just as long as Willis doesn't try any more of his tricks,' O'Rourke muttered darkly.

'He'd better not,' said Valin. 'And he'd better take good care of Maddox. If Willis turns up alone, I'm going to have a few words with him.'

'You won't be the only one,' said O'Rourke.

'Maddox is going to be unhappy about his mate,' said Angel. 'They've been together a long time.'

'Them's the breaks,' said Valin. 'He'll have to deal with it. All of us here have had to in the past.'

'You can say that again,' said Spenser.

They set off again in the direction of the back of the house, keeping a weather eye out for opposition, but meeting none, until they came to the kitchens, which were vast and deserted.

'Through here,' said Trudy, and led them past the ranks of industrial sinks and ovens big enough to cook a feast for an entire royal family. Washing-up had been abandoned and food was still cooking on unattended hobs, giving the place something of the air of the *Marie Celeste*. They passed through a set of doors into a concrete-clad corridor, from which rose a single flight of stairs.

'Bingo!' said Valin. 'At last.'

'Up there,' said Trudy, 'are the laird's quarters.'

'But of course you're coming with us,' said Valin.

'Do I have to?'

'I insist,' said Angel. 'The more pretty women,

the better.' And this time he winked at Carmen, who gave him a friendly scowl.

And slowly, in single file, Valin in the lead, and Trudy bringing up the rear in front of Angel, who couldn't help admiring the way her bottom moved under her tight, black uniform skirt, they began to climb the stairs.

At the top, as the man said, the shit hit the fan.

A force of soldiers were waiting in ambush, and they laid down a killing field of fire into the corridor in which Valin's men found themselves, at the top of the stairs. It was a miracle that they weren't wiped out where they stood, as bullets ploughed into the walls and ricocheted around in the confined space.

Carmen was creased by a 9mm bullet that chopped through the front of her winter clothes, sliced a line of blood along her side, ripped through the back, and embedded itself in the plaster behind her. O'Rourke was hit in the upper arm and Phillips in the guts. They all dropped down into the stairwell, dragging Phillips behind them, and returned fire. Spenser's Gatling did the most damage, as he saw his wife take a round, and he fired a complete belt of ammunition, five hundred rounds, in a sustained burst that left the barrel of the gun red-hot.

No other injuries were sustained, but Trudy fell to her knees screaming, as bullets flew and smoke and the smell of cordite filled the air.

When the smoke cleared, a pall of silence hung over the wreckage that Spenser had made of the corridor, only punctured by Phillips's moans of pain.

'Christ,' murmured Valin, as he looked at the survivors of the ambush. 'I don't believe this.'

Angel left Trudy sobbing soundlessly, and stuck his head over the edge of the top step.

Nothing.

He pulled himself up further.

Still nothing.

Finally he clambered up on to the landing, and went for a look-see.

The heavy shells from Spenser's Gatling had done their job, and Angel found seven bodies along the corridor. Good work, Spense, he thought, and went back to report his findings.

Spenser was kneeling by Carmen's side, putting a field-dressing on her wound, while Valin was trying to deal, to no avail, with the blood pouring from the wound in Phillips's stomach. Trudy, who seemed to have recovered again, was patching up O'Rourke's arm.

'We screwed them,' said Angel. 'How is everyone?'

Valin shook his head. Jesus Christ, thought Angel, we're going to lose this one, when suddenly he heard the rattle of automatic fire from below them. 'Maddox and Willis,' he said. 'The Lone Ranger and Tonto, riding to our rescue.'

'Well, at least it'll keep our friends occupied,' said Valin. 'There's nothing I can do for Phillips. The rest of you OK?'

Everyone nodded, if a little painfully, and Valin picked up his Uzi and said: 'Come on. We must be nearly there. Trudy?'

'Yes,' she confirmed. 'The master and mistress's suite is at the end of the corridor there. But do you mind if I don't come any further?'

'Why's that?' asked Valin, as if he couldn't guess.

'The master keeps his best men with him at all times. He's dreadfully scared of being assassinated. They work in shifts. I don't want to die.'

'Happy thoughts,' said O'Rourke, and he winced as pain shot down his arm.

'And you think that's what's going to happen to us?' asked Valin.

'I do. And I'm sorry.' She glanced at Angel, and her colour was high. 'Why don't you leave it? Take care of your friend?' She gestured at Phillips, who lay on the stairs, blood still oozing from his wound through his clothes and a white foam forming on his lips. Angel was kneeling beside him, unstrapping the radio from his back and transferring it to his own.

'We can't,' said Valin, as the sound of gunfire from beneath them became louder. 'And listen. The cavalry's coming.'

'You're all mad,' said Trudy, as everyone picked up their weapons.

'No,' said Valin. 'Not entirely. We took payment to do a job, and we intend to see it through. You stay here, Trudy. Do what you can for our friend, and good luck to you. Thanks for the help. Maybe we'll meet again.'

'I hope so,' said Angel, and gave her a salute as he fell in behind the others, leaving her and Phillips in the gloom of the stairwell.

'But you can't just leave him here,' protested Trudy. 'He'll die.'

'I'm sorry,' said Angel as he went. 'But he knew what he was letting himself in for when he joined us.'

They proceeded carefully down the corridor, guns at the ready. The place was silent except for the sporadic gunfire from below that seemed to be getting closer. And as the corridor widened, and the furnishings became more sumptuous, Valin realized they were approaching the hub of Robertson's small empire.

'Watch out for the Praetorian Guard,' he whispered to O'Rourke, who was following him closely.

'Do you think Stone is up here?' the younger man asked.

'You can count on it.'

And then the corridor opened into a huge hall

dominated by a set of hefty double doors, faced in dark-green leather, and they knew that they had arrived.

'Knock, knock,' said Angel.

'What's behind the green door?' sang Spenser in a whisper.

'Let's try it and see,' said Valin, and crouching down, he pushed down one of the gold-plated handles with the end of the barrel of his Uzi. The handle moved but the door didn't, and as he touched it, bullets thudded through the door at chest height, splintering wood, tearing the leather to shreds, and chopping holes in the plaster opposite.

Valin jumped back to the cover of the wall. 'Could've been nasty,' he said. 'Spenser. Deal with it.'

The American grinned, aimed his Gatling at the lock and let fly a long burst of high-explosive bullets.

The lock gave and the doors gaped slightly.

Valin leaned over and pushed open the one closest to him. There was more fire from inside, and the mercenaries moved back to avoid ricochets.

'Stalemate,' said Valin, his voice sounding strange in his own ears as they rang from the gunfire. 'We're outside, and they're inside, and never the twain shall meet.'

'We've got to do something,' said O'Rourke.

'Too true. I wonder what's happened to the other two.'

As if on cue, they heard more gunfire, even closer this time, then after a couple of minutes, a soft clatter from the corridor behind them. All guns turned in that direction as Maddox and Willis, both soaking wet, came sliding down towards them, using every doorway and piece of furniture as cover. Maddox had blood on his face, and a crude bandage wrapped round his head.

'You're OK,' he said, as the others lowered their weapons. 'We couldn't be sure. We met a wee girl on the stair, and she thought you'd copped it.'

'What happened to you?' Valin said to Maddox.

'Collected a stray one on the way up. You've stirred up a hornet's nest down below.'

'And how has our friend behaved?' Valin asked.

'Willis has been fine,' said Maddox, then his eyes narrowed. 'Where's Jackie?'

'He didn't make it,' said Valin. 'I'm sorry. He did a good job for us.'

'Oh Christ,' said Maddox. 'That's a bastard.'

'I know,' said Valin. 'There was nothing we could do.'

'Where is he?'

'We had to leave him.'

'I knew I should've come with you.'

'There wasn't anything you could have done. He walked into a shit storm.'

'I could've brought him out.'

'And got yourself killed.'

'We've been together for years. He was my mate.'

'I'm sorry,' said Valin again. 'But it happens to the best of men.' Then he changed the subject. 'How's Phillips?' he asked.

'Dead,' said a voice from the shadows. It was Trudy.

'You should've gone back down,' said Valin to the girl.

'Maybe,' she replied. 'But I think anyone going down would've been shot. Besides, I thought I might be able to help.'

'How? Can you use a gun?'

'No.'

'Well, that's the only kind of help we need right now. We're stuck out here, and we can't get inside. And we can't go back down without being blown to pieces. We're buggered, if you'll excuse my French.'

'There's another way,' said Trudy.

'What?' asked Valin.

'Through the attics,' she said, glancing upwards.

Valin followed her eyes. 'Of course. Very good, Trudy. I should've thought of that myself. How do we get up there?'

'I'll show you.'

'Good girl. Spenser, you and Carmen stay here with O'Rourke. I'll take Angel, Maddox and Willis over the top. Can you manage, Willis? With your arm?'

'Of course, sir.'

'Good man. Come on then, Trudy. Lead the way.'

They went back to one of the doorways they'd passed on the way to the hall. All around them the massive house was quiet. Trudy tried the door. It was locked. Valin stepped forward, gun in hand, prepared to blow off the lock, but she gestured to him to stay back and produced a small bunch of keys from one of the pockets of her skirt. 'This way no one will know we're inside if they get this far,' she said.

'Remind me to put you on the payroll,' said Valin as she opened the door.

They all passed through, and once inside, she locked it again behind them. They found themselves in another corridor, but this one was smaller and dustier than the others they'd passed through, and at the end was a narrow, bare staircase leading upwards.

'Best to take your boots off,' said Trudy. 'Just in case they hear us,' and she slipped her own low-heeled shoes off and carried them in one hand.

Valin and his men did the same, Willis requiring some help because of his wounded arm. The men slung their boots round their necks by the laces, and with Trudy leading the way they began to climb the stairs. It was not a long climb, and at the top they were faced with another door. This one was unlocked, and Trudy opened it, peered through, flashed back a smile and opened it fully.

Inside were revealed the attics of the house. They were thick with dust, full of piles of shadowy junk, and criss-crossed with sturdy joists supporting the ceilings of the halls and apartments below.

The group padded through the gloom and when they came to a trapdoor set into the floor Trudy held her finger to her lips and said: 'The bathroom to the master bedroom is under here.'

'How do you know?' asked Valin.

'Servants know everything about a house,' she replied. 'Don't you know that?'

'You're a treasure, Trudy,' Valin said, grinning.

He tried the handle of the trapdoor. It opened smoothly. Down below was yet more dim twilight, and he opened it fully.

'Anyone on the john?' whispered Angel.

Valin shook his head, and swiftly tugged on his boots. 'No,' he whispered back. 'But if there had been, they'd have had one hell of a shock.'

He handed his carry weapon to Angel and dropped down to the marble floor of the bathroom, took the weapon back, then helped the rest, as one by one they dropped down. He gestured for Trudy to come closer, and said: 'You stay in here. We're going to take a look-see.'

She grimaced at his words, but stayed put, as he gently opened the door between the bathroom and the master bedroom.

Valin peered out and found himself looking at a massive empty boudoir with a huge round bed in the centre, covered with a wine-red silk bedspread. He opened the door further, and when he was convinced no one was inside, pushed it all the way, and stepped into the next room.

The other three followed him. 'Nice pad,' said Angel, looking round. 'The honeymoon suite, do you think?'

'I don't know,' said Valin as he looked at the door in the wall opposite the bathroom. 'But I don't think the next room is going to be so quiet.'

At the front of the apartments, Spenser and his two companions could hear noise and movement from back the way they'd come. 'Looks like we've got company,' he said. 'Prepare to repel boarders.'

'Can't you ever be serious?' said O'Rourke.

'No, Mark,' replied Spenser, as he cocked his gun. 'I might just burst into tears.' And as a face and the barrel of a gun appeared around the corner of the corridor, a few yards from where it opened up into the hall, where he, Carmen and O'Rourke were standing, he fired off a burst that stripped the plaster down to the brickwork.

'Grenades,' said O'Rourke, and all three produced fragmentation grenades, pulled out the pins, armed them, and threw them in the direction that the enemy was coming from, before ducking down for cover behind the antique furniture that filled the hall. The grenades exploded as one, shaking the house to its foundations, and bringing down part of the ceiling of the corridor.

'That should keep them busy for a few minutes,'

said Spenser through a pall of dust, as firing started up from inside the apartments again, and did more damage to the double doors. 'And the local builder for at least a week.'

Inside the master bedroom, Valin and the rest heard the firing, followed by the noise and concussion from the grenades, and the sound of firing from closer to them, just a room or two away.

'Shit,' said Angel, as dust drifted down from their ceiling too. 'What the fuck've they got outside?'

'I hope it's our lot,' said Valin as he walked across the thick-pile carpet, and the door in front of him suddenly flew open and an armed soldier came running in. He stopped in astonishment, the door closing gently behind him. His mouth opened to shout a warning, and Angel fired a short burst from his suppressed Scorpion, and the soldier hit the floor, his blood staining the white carpet the same colour as the bedspread.

'Think he needed to use the Gents?' asked Willis, with a rare attempt at humour.

'Not no more,' said Angel, and changed magazines. 'Shall we move into the parlour, Colonel? Perhaps they'll offer us tea. They'll be expecting our boy back in a minute.' He gestured to the body on the floor. 'It'd be a shame to disappoint them.'

'After you then, Angel,' said the colonel.

Angel went to the door and opened it a fraction. Inside was a huge room, hung with the most valuable antiques yet, and Angel could see at least three people. Guarded by a soldier dressed in fatigues, holding a .45-calibre grease gun at port arms, were Dirk Robertson, looking pale and frightened, and with her back to him in an armchair, a woman with dark hair, whom Angel assumed to be Lord Petersham's daughter.

12

Angel let the door slip closed and communicated in a whisper what he'd seen to his commanding officer.

'Anyone else in there?' asked Valin

'Not that I could see.'

'Go for it, then. But be careful.'

'My pleasure, Colonel,' said Angel as he turned, checked that his carry weapon was cocked, and with one heavily booted foot kicked open the door and jumped into the room.

The soldier and Robertson, who was kitted out in full Highland dress, his heavy kilt in predominantly dark-green shades, both looked over as the door burst open, and the soldier tried to pull down his gun into a firing position. 'Leave it,' said Angel.

And then, from where he had been sitting, out of Angel's sight when he peered through the door, another armed soldier opened fire with an M16. The bullets narrowly missed the American, and he returned fire, dropping to the floor as he did so, slamming both the soldier and the seat back against the wall with a burst from his Scorpion.

Meanwhile the standing soldier fired too, his burst stitching a line along the wall and the door, driving the other three back into the bathroom, before Angel fired again, and got his second target dead on.

Valin walked into the room and Dirk Robertson looked coldly at him. Although he was still pale, he spoke with authority when he said, in a broad Scottish accent: 'What is the meaning of this intrusion? This invasion of private property? This shooting and killing? Who the hell are you?'

'My name is Colonel James Valin, late of the SAS, now in command of my own private force. We're here to rescue the woman you kidnapped.'

'Kidnapped. That's rubbish. She's here of her own free will.'

'That's not what we were told. We understand you are keeping her here against her wishes, and those of her father.'

'Then I suggest you ask her,' said Robertson.

The woman in the armchair, who had remained sitting through all the shooting and excitement, turned slowly and looked at the rest of the intruders as they bundled into the room. It was Lady Vanessa, and she was even better-looking than in the photo that Bryant-Marshall had supplied. 'Well, well,' she said wryly. 'My heroes.'

'Your ladyship,' said Valin with half a bow. 'We are at your service.'

'Then I suggest you take this raggle-taggle bunch and go back to wherever you came from.'

'Fuck off, in other words,' said Angel, who by that time had picked himself up off the floor, and had checked both the bodies for vital signs, of which there were none.

'Quite,' said Lady Vanessa, apparently totally unfazed by the invasion and the two dead bodies in the room.

Valin looked puzzled. 'Your ladyship,' he said, 'we have been paid a considerable sum of money to complete our mission. This thing went as high as Number Ten Downing Street. I have lost some good men. Some very good men. And Mr Robertson has lost a lot more. And now you're telling me we were sent on a wild-goose chase.'

'Precisely.' She leant over and took Robertson's hand and gave it a squeeze. 'I'm very happy staying here with my betrothed.'

Valin looked at Angel, who pulled a face.

'No,' said the colonel. 'I'm afraid we've come this far, done what needed to be done, and we don't intend to leave without you.'

'This *is* kidnapping,' cut in Robertson. 'And I won't have it.'

'You have no choice: we're taking the lady. Presumably you'll tell your men to hold their fire.'

Robertson looked as if he was about to froth at the mouth.

'Don't worry, Dirk,' said Lady Vanessa, 'I'm not

going anywhere. If they want to take me out of here, they'll have to do it bodily, with me kicking and screaming.'

'That can be arranged,' said Angel. And Lady Vanessa gave him a penetrating look.

'No.' They were interrupted by a female voice, as Trudy came out of the bathroom and placed herself defiantly between Valin and Lady Vanessa.

'What are *you* doing here, Trudy?' For the first time Lady Vanessa seemed surprised at the turn of events.

'I brought them through.'

'You did what?' shouted Robertson. 'You stupid little fool.'

'I didn't want any more people killed.'

'So what about these two? And Smiley?'

'Who's he?' asked Angel.

'The other soldier. He needed to use the bath-room.'

'His bathroom-using days are over,' said Valin crisply. 'Now, we'd like to get moving as soon as possible, and I believe you need to get a message through to your troop commander.'

'How much?' said Robertson after a moment, when he seemed to have calmed down slightly.

'I beg your pardon?' replied Valin.

'How much *were* you paid?'

'One million sterling.'

Robertson looked at Lady Vanessa. 'At least he thinks you're worth something,' he remarked.

'For the first time,' she replied.

Robertson looked at Valin. 'I'll match it.'

'You'll what?' said Valin incredulously.

'I'll match it. I'll give you a million to go away. I'll guarantee your free passage to whatever vessel brought you in. I can't say fairer.'

Valin smiled. 'Let me see the money,' he said.

The shrewd businessman in Robertson came out straight away. 'How do I know I can trust you?'

'How do I know I can trust *you*?' countered Valin.

Robertson drew himself up to his full, not inconsiderable height. 'As owner and Laird of Lochnercrag, and commander-in-chief of its army, believe me, you can take my word. As one gentleman to another.'

'Stow it, Robertson,' Maddox interrupted. 'You're no more than a wee bairn from the Gorbals, just like me. Listen to the voice on you, for God's sake. Don't come your airy-fairy ways with us. Now, you can trust us, or do the other. But then we'll take the girl whether she wants to come or not.'

'Well put,' said Valin.

'Very well,' said Robertson. 'I need to get to the safe.'

'Maddox, watch him,' ordered Valin. 'Make sure it's only money he gets out.'

'He's not so stupid as to try anything,' said Maddox. But all the same he moved closer to Robertson.

The laird went to a tartan wall-hanging of the same design as his kilt and drew it aside. Behind it was a large safe. He set the combination and opened the door. Maddox checked the inside and nodded to Valin. 'Just money,' he said. 'And lots of it.'

'Go ahead,' said the colonel, and Robertson began to transfer piles of banded notes from the safe to a nearby table. Eventually, when the tabletop had disappeared under paper money, he said: 'One million. A lot are Scottish banknotes, but I believe they spend just as well south of the border.'

'What's left?' Valin said to Maddox.

'A fair amount. And there *is* something else.' He put in his hand and withdrew it, holding a soft-leather pouch. He opened the top and tipped out the contents on to the pile of money. Hundreds of diamonds made a twinkling counterpoint to the notes on to which he poured them.

'A sideline?' asked Valin.

'Just part of a business deal,' replied Robertson.

'How much are they worth?'

Robertson shrugged. 'A lot.'

'I'm sure. Have you a bag for the money?' said Valin.

Robertson went into the master bedroom with Maddox, and they came out with an expensive suitcase into which Robertson put the money.

'And the rest,' said Valin. 'Including the sparklers.'

'No.'

'I'm sorry,' said Valin. 'The spoils of war.'

'You gave me your word.'

'No,' said Valin. 'I just asked how I knew I could trust you.'

'You bastard.'

'*And* we're taking the girl.'

'*What*?'

'You are naïve, Dirk,' said Lady Vanessa. 'But I won't go easily.'

'Then we'll dose you up with morphine and carry you out,' said Valin. 'Make up your mind. The easy way or the hard way. It's of no consequence to us.'

'You're swine, all of you,' said Lady Vanessa hotly.

'Well?' asked Valin again.

'I'll go with you.' She sounded resigned to her fate, but Valin took it with a pinch of salt.

'Then I'm coming too,' said Trudy.

'Quite a party,' said Angel, and winked at Trudy. 'I'll find you a place to stay if you like, when we get back to London.'

Trudy reddened under his gaze. 'Don't be cheeky,' she said.

'I think you'd better warn your men off,' said Valin to Robertson, realizing he was lucky that no one had come through to check on their boss while the negotiations had been taking place. 'Maddox, you seem to be able to handle him best. You go with him.'

'A pleasure, chief,' said the Scot. 'Come on now, wee man. Let's get busy.'

Robertson scowled at Maddox, but went to the door opposite the one to the bedroom and opened it. 'Men,' he said. 'Lay down your guns. We're prisoners.'

Inside the room, which opened into a hallway where the leather-clad door was situated – and thus to where Spenser, Carmen and O'Rourke were waiting for something to happen, nothing having occurred since they let off the grenades – were half a dozen uniformed soldiers, led by an officer with captain's stars on his uniform. As Robertson spoke, and the captain saw the filthy, bedraggled figure of Maddox behind him, he moved the Colt Commander he was holding in his right hand in a slow arc towards the pair of them.

'You heard the man,' said Maddox, placing the barrel of his pump-action shotgun against Robertson's neck. 'Put the bloody guns down, or I'll blow his wee head to hell.'

One by one the men put their weapons on the floor, and Maddox pushed Robertson inside. The other three followed him, bringing Lady Vanessa with them, collected the soldiers' guns and piled them in one corner, as far away from their prisoners as they could get. Willis then disarmed the weapons by removing the magazines and clearing the actions.

'That's better,' said Valin, when this had been

done. 'Willis, get Spenser and the rest in here. But be careful. They shoot first, and ask questions later.'

Willis carefully walked, halfway to the door, then yelled out: 'Spenser. It's me, Toby. We're in control in here. Don't shoot.'

'Show yourself,' Spenser called back, not sure he could tell the Englishman's voice from another. 'Come on out. I want to be sure.'

Willis eased the double doors open, and stuck out his head. The Gatling and O'Rourke's Scorpion were trained on the door.

'It's OK, chaps,' he said. 'We've got them. The girl and all. Now come in quick, so we can secure this door.'

The trio outside approached, and looked carefully over Willis's shoulder in case of tricks, but when they saw Robertson's soldiers, kneeling on the carpet with their hands above their heads, Robertson himself, and Lady Vanessa all huddling together like refugees, and the remainder of their own comrades all still carrying their weapons, they went inside, and Maddox and Angel manhandled a huge dresser in front of the door.

'That should keep everything copacetic for a while,' said Valin, and quickly explained what they had missed to Spenser, Carmen and O'Rourke. Then he said: 'Willis, go and keep an eye on that trapdoor in the bathroom. If Trudy knows about it, so do others, and it's only a matter of time before someone tries to use it.'

'Sir,' said Willis, and doubled off on his mission.

'Spenser, watch the front doors. Maddox, you watch the laird and his lady. Carmen, until you're needed, stay with Trudy. Angel, I may live to regret this, but you take charge of the money and the diamonds. And Angel . . .'

'Colonel.'

'Just make sure none of them go astray.'

'Colonel. As if.'

'I know. I'm just a suspicious old bastard, but I always like to make things clear early on. No offence meant.'

'None taken, sir. Trust me.'

'Sure. You're a doctor. Now, Mark, we need to talk.'

They conferred in a corner.

'What's this about her wanting to stay?' asked O'Rourke immediately.

'Seems like someone got the wrong end of the stick. She's in love with him. They want to get married.'

'And?'

'And tough. We take her out, deliver her back to Bryant-Marshall, collect the balance of our fee, split it, and the money and gems from here, and lie low for a while.'

'I wish it was as easy as you make it sound, Colonel. But Stone is still on the loose out there somewhere.'

'Don't worry. We'll soon sort that,' said Valin.

Then, raising his voice, he said: 'Mr Robertson, come here will you, please. I need a word.'

Robertson joined the pair. 'How do you communicate with outside?' asked Valin.

'By phone. Satellite-linked portable, or land-line.'

'Good. And where is Mr Stone?'

'I don't know.'

'Just outside the door, I imagine,' said Valin. 'Call him, there's a good chap, and get him to surrender to us.'

'Christ, Colonel,' said O'Rourke. 'He'll never surrender.'

'On the personal order of his C-in-C, I think he will. That man's got discipline tattooed on his forehead.'

'I hope you're right. Now, Robertson, the phone.'

Reluctantly Robertson picked up the instrument and keyed in a number. It was answered in a second.

'Roland, they have us,' said Robertson. 'Order your men to put down their weapons.' There was a pause. 'You heard me, Roland,' the laird said harshly. 'I repeat, they have us all, including Vanessa, and they're coming out. Under no circumstances do I want any gunfire. They must be allowed to go back to the shore unmolested. Now, do you understand me?' Another pause. 'Good,' said Robertson, and put down the receiver.

He turned to Valin and said: 'You're free to go, Colonel.'

'Thank you,' said Valin, then to Lady Vanessa: 'Your ladyship, you'll need warm clothes.'

'I'll go as I am.' She was dressed in a light sweater and thin trousers, with a pair of leather pumps on her feet.

'No. Once again you have a choice. Either dress yourself warmly, or one of us will dress you.'

Lady Vanessa scowled, and Trudy said: 'I'll help, ma'am.'

'Very well. It seems I have no choice.'

'We have to go to the bedroom,' said Trudy.

'Carmen, will you accompany the ladies?' said Valin, and Carmen nodded in reply.

When they had left, Valin turned to Robertson and said tersely: 'You'd better get some warm clothes on too. You're coming with us.'

'How far?'

'As far as the harbour to secure our safe passage out of here. Don't worry, we aren't going to take you any further. You weren't part of the original contract.'

'I'll get my coat.'

'When the others have finished,' said Valin. 'And we'll need transport.'

'Yeah,' said Spenser over his shoulder. 'The vehicle we came in on is kind of the worse for wear.'

'There are plenty available,' said Robertson.

'Maybe we'd better have one waiting for us

outside the front door,' said Valin. 'How about arranging that. And you'd better tell your man you're coming with us, just in case he has any tricks up his sleeve. I'll personally make sure you get it first if he does.'

Once again Robertson keyed a number on his portable phone and spoke to Stone through tight lips. 'I'll need a jeep outside to take us to the harbour,' he said. 'And I'm accompanying the party, so let's have no surprises,' he forced himself to add.

'Good,' said Valin. 'Co-operation. That's what I like to see.'

At that point, the three women came back. Trudy and Lady Vanessa were now both wearing winter clothing – a mishmash of what they could find: ski suits, heavy sweaters and leather coats and boots. Some of it, from its size, appeared to belong to Robertson.

'Get your coat,' said Valin to the laird.

Robertson went into the bedroom too, accompanied by Maddox, and when he was warmly wrapped up in a thick, fleecy-lined leather coat and matching gloves, the party got ready to leave the apartment.

Spenser left first, with his Gatling at the ready, and Carmen beside him. Then came Valin with Robertson and Maddox. Angel was next, carrying the bag of money and precious gems. He was followed by Lady Vanessa and Trudy, covered by

O'Rourke. Willis brought up the rear, and as they left he collected the radio that Angel had dumped behind a sofa in the hall before they had set off through the attics.

There was no sign of anyone as they walked past the debris of the gunfights, and along the deserted hall to the main staircase that led down to where Bryant had been killed.

When they came to the main door, which was riddled with bullet holes from Spenser's Gatling and Phillips's Uzi, Valin said: 'Well, here goes. Good luck, everyone.' He twisted the heavy knob and pulled the door open. Outside it was nearly dark, evening coming quickly in that part of the world, and it seemed impossible that they'd been so long on the island. It was freezing outside. The wind was at its height, and blew snow almost horizontally on to the many inches that already coated the courtyard.

In front of the house, next to the wreckage of the Suzuki they'd hijacked from the harbour, was a similar vehicle, painted fire-engine red. The tracks made by its oversized tyres were dark against the snow, but even they were beginning to fill in.

'Let me go,' O'Rourke said, and stepped out on to the porch and down the three, slippery, snow-covered steps and across to the car, his feet sinking deeply into the drift. He felt terribly vulnerable as he went, expecting at any moment to feel the thud of bullets as they cut him down before he heard the sound of the shots.

The Suzuki was empty, the keys were in the ignition, and all seemed well, so he gestured for the rest to join him. He knew this was the time that if something was going to happen, it would, but the whole place remained quiet as one by one they climbed in and Angel took the wheel. It was a tight squeeze, but an extra row of seats had been fitted at the back, so they managed it.

The engine started first time. It was already in four-wheel drive, and Angel started the wipers and switched on the lights full beam before he slowly pulled away.

The drive back to the harbour, in the gathering darkness, took even longer than the drive up, and about halfway there Valin told Willis to start calling the submarine on the radio.

Willis extended the aerial as far as it would go in the confined interior of the vehicle and switched on the set. He put on the headphones, stuck the mouthpiece to his lips, and turned the dial at the front. 'Gosling to Mother Goose,' he intoned. 'Come in, please.'

In his ears he heard nothing but a heavy burst of static.

'Gosling to Mother Goose,' he said again. 'Do you read? Come in, please.'

More static.

Willis tugged off the cans and said: 'Nothing. Must be the weather.'

'Damn,' growled Valin.

'Could be better when we get close,' said Spenser.

'I hope so,' said Angel from the driver's seat. 'The last thing we want to be is waiting at that harbour all night, freezing our nuts off, with our thumbs up our asses . . . Sorry, ladies.'

'You have a talent for finding the nub of a problem, Angel,' said Valin. 'And you're quite right.'

'We'll have to hole up in that blockhouse,' said O'Rourke. Turning to Maddox and Willis, he said: 'What was the state of those guards when you left?'

'The guy the colonel killed was still dead. The others were still tied up,' answered Maddox drily. 'But they could've got loose.'

'We'll have to watch out for them, then,' said Valin.

'Except the dead guy,' said Angel.

'Quite,' said Valin.

Then Angel felt the road dip, and he knew they were on the last leg of the short journey, as the road started to descend finally to sea level, and he slowed even more. 'Soon be there, sir,' he told Valin.

'Keep an eye out, everyone,' said the colonel. 'We don't know what hotheads there are about, looking to avenge their mates.'

But everything remained quiet, and a few minutes

later Angel drew up beside the hulk of the snow-covered Suzuki they'd destroyed earlier, close to the door of the blockhouse.

'Mark,' said Valin, 'you and Angel have a look inside. Angel, leave the bag with me. Willis, try the radio again. This time from outside. Spenser, Carmen, cover the way we came in case we were followed. Maddox and I will stay in here and look after our guests. All of you be very careful.'

The five of them went about their allotted tasks, and Valin slid behind the wheel. The engine was still running to both keep the heater going and facilitate a quick getaway if necessary. Not that there were a lot of places to go: just a short run down to the harbour before finally coming up dead to the relentless, grey water.

Spenser and Carmen took cover behind the frozen, burnt-out Suzuki, and both squinted through the snow for signs of pursuit. Willis went close to the sea wall, switched on the radio again and sent out the call sign, as Angel gently opened the door to the blockhouse. Inside all seemed to be quiet. He pulled a face at O'Rourke, and led the way up the stairs. It was cold up there, as if the heating had been turned off, and fresh air blew through the open doorway at the top of the stairs.

Angel turned and pulled another face. It seemed highly unlikely that Maddox and O'Rourke would have opened any windows before they left. At least not without mentioning it a moment or two earlier. It was even colder in the radio room, but the freezing air coming through the open window did little to hide the stench of death that pervaded the place. Not just the death of the soldier that Valin had executed earlier, but also of the other four guards, who lay stiffly, still trussed like chickens, each with a neat bullet hole in the back of his head.

'Jesus,' said Angel. 'What the fuck happened here?'

'Christ knows,' replied O'Rourke. 'We'd better search the rest of the place. Whoever did it might still be around.'

'Pleasant thought,' said Angel, and his finger stroked the trigger of his Scorpion.

They went right through the rest of the block-house together. It was empty.

'You wanna go tell the colonel,' said Angel, when they got back to the radio room, and he'd shut the window. 'I'll try and fix the heating. And get someone up here to help me shift these stiffs out of the way, will you. We don't want those civilians seeing this mess.'

'They'll smell it anyway,' said O'Rourke, and went downstairs, gun at the ready, to the Suzuki.

Valin powered down the window at his signal. 'Speak to you, sir?' said O'Rourke. 'In private.'

Valin's eye narrowed, as he closed the window and stepped out into the keening wind and driving snow.

O'Rourke explained what he and Angel had found, to which Valin said: '*All* dead?'

'Sir. Executed.'

'Who did it? Any ideas?'

'Who knows? Must've been someone from the house. Maybe Stone got miffed at the easy way they were taken and did a field court martial and summary execution. It's his style, from what I've heard.' And yours, he thought privately.

'Then why isn't he still here?' asked Valin, as if he didn't expect an answer.

'God knows. But I need an able-bodied man to help Angel move the bodies if we're going to bivouac in there,' said O'Rourke. 'I don't think my arm's quite up to it yet.'

'Of course. I'll send Maddox.'

'The place reeks, sir. You'd better warn that lot. But there's nowhere else to go, and there's a more powerful radio up there – with a bigger range to contact the submarine. And maybe some hot food.'

'Fine. Tell the rest. And see if Willis has made contact yet.'

'Will do.'

O'Rourke vanished into the blizzard as Valin climbed back into the Suzuki.

'Maddox,' he said. 'Go upstairs. There's a nasty job needs doing. I'll be all right down here with this lot. And watch out for yourself.'

'Of course, sir,' replied Maddox, and got out of the truck.

'We'll be staying here for a while,' said Valin to Robertson, Lady Vanessa and Trudy. 'Something rather unpleasant has taken place upstairs. But we have no choice but to go inside until we contact our passage out of here. I'm sorry, but that's the way it goes sometimes.'

'What kind of unpleasant?' asked Lady Vanessa.

'I think any civilized person would call it murder,' said Valin in reply.

O'Rourke stumbled through the snow to the sea wall, where Willis was still trying to contact the sub. When O'Rourke tapped him on the shoulder, he looked up and pulled the phones off his ears. 'Any luck?' asked the lieutenant.

'Not so far.'

'Where the fuck are they?'

'Christ knows, I don't.'

'The colonel was right. This *is* a fucking shambles.'

Willis shrugged.

'You can go inside if you want,' said O'Rourke wearily. 'It'll be warmer in there.'

'Thank Christ. I'm freezing my nuts off out here.'

'By the way.'

'What?'

'How were the prisoners when you left them?'

'Fine. Why?'

'You didn't think that it might be safer if they were dead?'

'Jesus, no. Why?'

'Guess.'

'They're not . . .'

O'Rourke nodded.

'But how?'

'Executed. A single bullet, back of the head.'

'It wasn't us, I swear. We left together, and they were still alive.'

'Sure.'

'Let me see.'

The two men made their way to the blockhouse.

Maddox had got there first, and his amazement seemed as genuine as Willis's. 'Jesus,' he said, when he found Angel standing beside the bodies, the heating system, which was now working, making the smell even worse. 'What happened?'

'You tell me,' said the American.

'You don't think I had anything to do with this, do you? I'm a fucking soldier – not a murderer. I kill people, sure, but not like this.'

'What, never?' asked Angel coolly, as they picked up the first stiff body and carried it through to a storeroom at the back of the building.

Maddox looked at him hard. 'Maybe once or twice I've done things I didn't like. But not today.'

'I believe you,' said Angel. 'But someone sure as hell killed these guys in cold blood.'

As they returned for the second body they heard footsteps on the stairs and picked up their weapons, only to put them down again when O'Rourke and Willis came in.

'Shit,' said O'Rourke. 'You'll have to open the window again.'

'My God,' said Willis, looking at the remaining three bodies. 'Maddox, am I going crazy?'

'No,' replied the Scot. 'Someone's been here since we left.'

Within a few minutes the other bodies had been stashed away, and with the window open again, the smell of death began to dissipate slightly. O'Rourke said: 'I'll go and get the rest. Willis, try the other radio. We've got to contact that sub and get out of here. Our luck's going to run out soon if we're not careful. I can feel it.'

Willis nodded, went to the big transceiver and switched it on.

'Gosling to Mother Goose,' he said slowly into the mike when he hit the right frequency. 'Do you read? Come in, please.'

O'Rourke went back to the vehicle and told Valin he could bring the others in, and then when they were safely inside, went and fetched Spenser and Carmen.

At the top of the stairs, Lady Vanessa blanched. 'What's that terrible smell?' she said.

'Dead meat,' said Angel. 'Come on in. The water's fine.'

'What happened here?' demanded Robertson. 'Where are my men?'

'Someone killed them,' said Angel.

'Who?'

'Who knows?'

'Let me see them.'

The American looked at Valin, who nodded. 'This way,' said Angel, and he and Maddox took Robertson into the storeroom.

The laird went white when he saw the five bodies, four still tied up tightly. 'Did you do this?' he said sharply.

'Only the one,' said Angel. 'That was an act of war. The other four were murdered where they lay.'

'But not by you.'

Angel shook his head.

'And you expect me to believe that?'

'Believe what you want.'

'You're nothing but a bunch of cold-blooded killers.'

Angel shook his head again.

'You bastard,' said Robertson, and made a move.

Angel hit him with the barrel of his Uzi. 'I said we didn't do it,' he rasped. 'Why the fuck should I bother to lie?'

13

After the umpteenth call to the sub, Willis got a reply. 'Mother Goose to Gosling,' a voice boomed through the speakers. 'Receiving you strength ten. Come in, please. Over.'

'Gosling to Mother Goose. Receiving you strength ten also. Where the hell have you been? I've been calling you for nearly an hour. Over.'

'Sorry, Gosling. Something else came up. Our apologies. What is your status?'

'Our status is mission accomplished with three deceased, and slight injuries to three more. The lady is ours.'

'Congratulations. What is your location? Over.'

'We are in the blockhouse overlooking the harbour. What is your location? Over.'

'We are twenty minutes out from you by surface craft. The weather is getting worse. We'll send an inflatable. Over.'

'We need seating for nine. We're bringing out one extra body. Over.'

'Understood, Gosling. We'll be with you directly. Over.'

'The sooner the better. But be careful. There may be bandits around. Understood? Over.'

'Understood, Gosling. We'll be spotting for them. Over and out.'

Willis spun round in his seat, and looked at the rest of them. 'Bingo!' he said. 'We'll be off this God-forsaken rock in half an hour.'

'Good man,' said Valin, as Angel and Maddox came back in with Robertson, who had a livid bruise coming up under the lump on his forehead.

'What did you do?' screamed Lady Vanessa as she ran to him.

'He decided to get physical,' said Angel. 'I had to pacify him.'

'They're murdering scum,' croaked Robertson. 'And I'll see them all in prison for this.'

'I'm terrified,' said O'Rourke, looking at his watch. 'We'd better forget the refreshments. We'll have to go in a few minutes.'

'You got through to the sub?' said Angel.

'Just now. They're twenty minutes away, and they're sending an inflatable.'

'That's the best news I've heard since our buddy here kindly opened his safe. I hope you've taken good care of the bag, Colonel. My retirement's in there.'

'No problem,' replied Valin.

'Are we going, sir?' said O'Rourke impatiently. 'I'd rather be early for our appointment than late.

Besides, we don't know who might be hanging around at the bus stop.'

'Well put, Mark,' said Valin. 'We don't indeed. OK, saddle up, people. We're on our way. Just one more short journey, Mr Robertson, and then we'll leave you alone.'

'Dirk,' pleaded Lady Vanessa. 'Isn't there anything you can do?'

Robertson made no reply.

Once again they all trooped out into the weather. Angel and O'Rourke went first to check the terrain. Not that there was a lot to see, as it was by then completely dark, and the storm seemed to be raging even harder.

'All clear, folks,' said Angel as he returned to the blockhouse. 'But keep an eye out. And for Christ's sake stay together. If we lose anyone out there, it could be for good.'

He saw Lady Vanessa exchange glances with Robertson, and said caustically: 'But don't get excited, Lady V. We'll make sure you don't stray. You're worth too much to us alive and well.'

They stayed close together as they headed down towards the harbour by the light of the torches that the navy had supplied with their kit, Lady Vanessa, Robertson and Trudy bunched in the middle. But even that close it was hard to communicate, as the biting wind blew the words out of their mouths when they spoke.

But finally, they came to the jetty that poked

out into the relatively quiet waters of the harbour, before it funnelled out into the open sea, where the waves roared and beat against the rocky shelf of Lochnercrag.

There was no sign of the inflatable from the submarine, and Valin looked at his watch. It was exactly fifteen minutes since they'd got the radio message.

'Five minutes to go,' he shouted, and then Maddox's head exploded like a water melon hit by a sledgehammer, showering them with red and grey pulp, and he fell over the edge of the jetty into the water with a dull splash, then disappeared under the waves. A split second later they heard the sound of a single shot, and then, through a megaphone, a voice said, in words whipped by the wind: 'Lay down your arms and you'll be unharmed. Otherwise you'll be shot down where you stand, like your companion.'

Valin's group fell into the snow, dragging Robertson, Lady Vanessa and Trudy with them. Valin put his mouth close to Robertson's ear and said: 'I promised you, you'd be first. Now get this sorted, or you're a dead man.'

They both got up slowly, Valin using Robertson as a shield, and after a dig in the back from the colonel's Uzi, the laird spoke. 'Don't shoot,' he shouted. 'There are innocent people here.'

'You will not be harmed, sir. But I have the

invaders covered. Now tell them to surrender or they will die.' It was Stone.

Valin knew it was a stalemate. If they fought back now, out in the open, it could only end in a massacre. And the civilians would probably die too, whatever the American promised. He knew that he and his troops were in an impossible situation, and he saw that Robertson knew it too, as the Scot turned with a look of triumph on his face. 'Are you going to kill us all in cold blood?' he asked. 'Like my men back at the blockhouse.'

Valin shook his head. 'We're not murderers,' he said. 'How many times do we have to tell you that?' And he placed his carry weapon down in the snow. 'Lay down your weapons,' he said to his party. 'We don't stand a chance.'

But the navy were on their way, he told himself. That was the half inch they were living in. And if they could only stay alive a little longer, perhaps the tables could be turned again.

'*Sir*,' complained Angel.

'Do it,' said Valin. 'I'm in command here.'

Everyone did as he told them, stood up, and raised their hands in the air. Within a minute, half a dozen figures appeared through the snow, two of them carrying high-powered sniper rifles, fitted with infrared and heat-seeking sights. At the head of the group was Stone, carrying the megaphone in one hand, a grease gun in the other.

'Valin,' he said. 'I knew it had to be you. Now

everyone take off their side-arms and add them to the pile. And no accidents. They could be fatal – for you. My men are none too happy about what's been going on here today.'

Once again everyone obeyed, and Stone said: 'Good.' Then to Robertson: 'Now, sir. Please bring her ladyship and Trudy and join us.'

Robertson did as he said, but first he picked up the case of money and jewels. 'My property, I think,' he said triumphantly.

'Now let's move into the windbreak over there,' said Stone, gesturing to his left. 'And we can talk.'

Everyone moved over towards the boat that had been pulled up on to a dry dock, where the wind and snow were less harsh. 'So what's to be done?' Stone said when they were there.

'Shoot them down where they stand,' ordered the laird, who seemed to have grown fully three inches taller since the raid had been thwarted. 'And be quick. They're due to be picked up any moment.'

'And you accused *us* of murder,' said Valin, staring at Robertson.

'Who *is* picking you up?' said Stone, ignoring the remark and looking out to sea.

'Wouldn't you like to know,' said Valin.

'Just another bunch of bloody pirates, I expect,' said Robertson. 'Now do it. Shoot them. Or do I have to do it for you?'

'Normally, of course, I wouldn't sanction such a thing,' said Stone mildly. 'But executing four

131

prisoners while they're tied hand and foot – now that's beyond the pale, as you Brits would say. And most unlike you too, James, if I may say so. Times must have changed.'

'It wasn't us,' protested Valin. 'How many times have I got to say it? We thought it was you.'

'What? Kill my own men? You can't be serious. I had forty-one soldiers here this morning. Forty-two, including me. Now I have half a dozen not killed or wounded. You cut a swathe, James, you and your men. And at what loss to you?'

'Four dead. Including the one you just shot. Three slightly wounded.'

'I thought it would be something like that. I have to congratulate you. But under the circumstances, did you really think I would kill four of my own?'

Valin didn't reply.

'Then who the hell *did* do it?' asked O'Rourke.

'It was me,' said a voice through the blizzard, and Jason McCall, who had last been seen floating away from O'Rourke's inflatable after falling overboard, appeared, carrying an M16 which he must have liberated from the block-house. As Stone's men turned in his direction, he fired one vicious burst that cut down two of them where they stood. 'Put up your weapons,' he said to the rest of them. 'Or you're dead.'

For one heart-stopping second it looked as if a gun battle might break out, but at a nod from Stone,

one by one, him included, they dropped their carry weapons into the snow.

Valin's men rescued them and their own, and ordered Stone and his soldiers to hit the ground. 'What the hell happened to you?' asked Willis.

'I nearly drowned,' said McCall. 'Thanks for searching for me so hard.'

'We truly thought you were a goner,' said O'Rourke.

'No thanks to you that I wasn't. But I managed to make the headland, and I found a sort of path up to the top. I nearly died from exposure, but there was a croft on the top, and I made a fire. There were even a few old cans of food in a cupboard.'

'It's a miracle,' said Willis.

'Thanks for your timely intervention,' said Valin. 'But why did you top the prisoners in the block-house?'

'I didn't know what the hell was happening. There was a burnt-out truck outside, and I didn't know what your casualties were.'

'You could have asked,' said Valin calmly.

'They were the enemy,' said McCall. 'Why should I believe what they said? And I didn't want them getting loose. One of them nearly was.'

'Why did you leave? Why not just stay there?' asked Willis.

'I walked up to the house. I saw you driving down, but I didn't know it was you. And then this lot . . .' – he gestured at the men on the floor

– 'followed. I saw that there'd been a heavy-duty battle up there, and decided to get back and try and get a message through to the sub. There were still some soldiers up there, though they didn't exactly look match-fit. I knew you'd done some damage, but I didn't know how much, and I could hardly ask.'

'Well, thank God you did,' said Willis. 'Otherwise we'd all be up shit creek now.'

'What do we do with this lot?' asked Angel, nodding at the prisoners.

'We're not going to kill them,' said Valin. 'We'll just leave them here with Robertson when the boat from the sub arrives.'

'If it ever does,' said O'Rourke, peering through the snow, out to sea.

And then it did. Through the storm, the waiting men and women on the jetty saw a bright-orange shape materialize through the darkness, swiftly followed by another, and the vessels negotiated the entrance of the harbour and hove to in its gentler waters.

They stayed back, as far out of gun range as possible, aimed the powerful searchlights that were mounted on the prow of each boat on to the jetty, and hailed the waiting group through a megaphone. 'Ahoy there,' came a voice from one of the boats. 'Identify yourselves.'

'Colonel James Valin and party,' Valin called back, through the megaphone he'd liberated from

Stone. 'With prisoners and Lord Petersham's daughter, Lady Vanessa.'

'Hold on, we're coming in,' said the voice, and the two inflatables moved closer.

There were two men in each vessel, and as they nudged the jetty, one jumped out from each and secured the boat to the bollards. When both were securely tied up, the two pilots disembarked, and Valin saw that one of them was the young lieutenant who had met them at the airfield. 'Good afternoon, sir,' he said to Valin. 'Or is it evening? Sorry about that, but we could hardly see our hands in front of our faces out there, and we didn't want to bump into any unfriendlies. So who do we have here?' He studied the new faces in the group, and the men lying face down under the guns of Angel and O'Rourke.

'May I introduce Lady Vanessa, her maid Trudy, and the so-called Laird of Lochnercrag, Dirk Robertson,' said Valin. 'And our prisoners are Roland Stone and the last survivors of his garrison here on the island.'

'You've done well,' said the lieutenant. 'But I suggest we get out of here as soon as possible. Now who exactly is coming with you?'

'Lady Vanessa and Trudy. The rest can stay here.'

'Who exactly are you?' Lady Vanessa asked the lieutenant.

'Sub-lieutenant Charles McGough,' replied the young officer.

'Lieutenant,' she said haughtily. 'I must vehemently protest at this invasion of privacy, and the murder of Mr Robertson's employees. I demand that you leave me here on the island, and arrest these men.' She looked at Valin and his companions.

'I'm sorry, your ladyship,' said McGough. 'But I have my orders. Now if you'd care to embark, we'll get back to my mother ship as soon as possible.'

'You can't do this,' blustered Robertson, as Valin and his team prepared to leave. 'I won't let you.'

'You don't have much choice,' said the colonel. 'Unless you'd rather die.'

'You're very brave with a gun in your hand,' said the Scot.

'I must confess to having found it easier that way,' replied Valin. 'But sadly we haven't time for a philosophical conversation right now, I'm afraid.' Then, with a smile, he picked up the suitcase of cash and diamonds. 'Our property, I think,' he said to Robertson.

'Bastard,' spat Lady Vanessa.

'We'll meet again,' said Stone from his prone position on the ground.

'I have no doubt,' said Valin. 'But for now it must be *au revoir*, if not goodbye . . . Ladies.'

Valin gallantly helped Lady Vanessa into one of the inflatables and Trudy into the other, and after throwing the captured weapons into the sea, the rest of the party squeezed themselves into the available seating, the pilots started the engines, the ratings cast off, and the boats turned and headed for the open sea again, leaving Robertson, Stone and the surviving soldiers peering after them through the murk.

Outside the harbour, the sea was high and wild, but McGough assured his passengers that the submarine was waiting just a few minutes away. Which it was, being tossed like a matchstick by the waves.

The sailors secured the inflatables with help from more ratings from on board, and Valin's party made the difficult transition from the small boats to the slippery deck of the large one, and went below with the pilots, leaving the sailors to bring in the satellite craft and stow them away.

The commander of the submarine was waiting for the colonel in the ward-room, as the others were led to their quarters, Lady Vanessa demanding to see someone in authority immediately, which McGough said she would in due course. 'What happened?' asked Valin when he saw the commanding officer. As he stripped off his soaking jacket, he went on: 'Where the hell were you? We were calling for hours. We could've been killed on that damned island. I thought you were supposed to be constantly monitoring our frequency.'

'Something came up,' said the commander.

'Like what?'

'Like a matter of national security. We had to take a look.'

'What are you talking about?'

'Someone's hijacked an oil rig is what I'm talking about,' replied the sailor. 'And we were the closest vessel.'

'Who?'

'A German named Jost. Eric Jost. You may have heard of him.'

'I have. My God, he's mad. This is serious.'

'I'll say it is.'

'And what's being done?'

'A platoon of commandos are being flown in from Northern Ireland to recapture the rig.'

'I don't fancy their chances. A platform like that will be easy to defend, and hard to take back by force.'

'We realize that, Colonel. But happily it's not one of your concerns.'

Just then there was a knock on the door, and a young rating with radio operator's badges on his sleeve came in with a flimsy. 'Sorry, sir,' he said to the commander, 'but this is urgent.'

The commander took the message, and as he read it his face darkened. He picked up the phone and dialled a two-digit number. 'McGough. In here now,' he barked.

'Bad news,' asked Valin

'The worst,' replied the commander. 'The army chopper has gone down in the sea with all hands.'

14

The hijack had gone as smoothly as it had been planned. The oil rig was like a big, fat plum, hanging on a tree, waiting to be picked. And pick it they did, as dawn broke through the lashing storm on the same November day as Valin and his men invaded Lochnercrag.

There were nine of them, led by one of the most wanted men in recent history. His name was Eric Jost, ex-Baader-Meinhof, and known to terrorists and their hunters the world over as 'The Mourner'. He was tall, slim and with blond hair, cut very short. His eyes were blue and penetrating, and he smoked constantly. On one wrist he had a tattoo of a man in prayer before a tombstone. Hence his nickname. His only other identifying feature was a birthmark in the shape of a strawberry on his right shoulder.

He had killed perhaps fifty men and women in a career which well justified his pseudonym, and he was totally ruthless in his desire to wreak havoc on society.

With him was his second in command, a massive Frenchman, Pierre Bernais, who was a veteran of the 1968 riots in Paris, and every other major political and social upheaval since, plus seven other terrorists, misfits, psychopaths and murderers. A hand-picked gang of cutthroats who would do anything for money, and if money wasn't forthcoming, would do anything for the sheer hell of it.

Jost sent out a mayday message from the powerful trawler that was carrying the gang to the rig, at ten hundred hours, and the radio operator on Northern Petroleum's oil rig Alpha Bravo Discovery immediately invited them to moor alongside, and transfer the three injured men that the message said were aboard, casualties of the weather, for casualty evacuation by helicopter to the mainland.

The trawler hove to fifteen minutes later, and three stretchers were lowered to its deck, with two paramedics to oversee the evacuation. The paramedics were knocked unconscious, and two terrorists put on their distinctive, lime-green fluorescent jackets and hats. Under the jackets they carried heavy-calibre handguns. Three more terrorists, armed with sub-machine-guns, were put on the stretchers, their weapons hidden under the blankets, and on the signal from the boat, were hauled aboard, with the bogus paramedics in attendance. As soon as they were safely on board, they all produced their guns, and took prisoner the astonished oil rig workers who had come to help the injured men.

Within a few minutes the terrorists had captured

the control and radio rooms, preventing the radio operator from sending any further messages to the mainland, and taken control of the helipad and helicopter, as the other five hijackers swarmed on to the platform. A quarter of an hour later, with no casualties to the invaders, and one dead and two wounded men on the rig, the coup was complete.

Jost went to the radio shack, as the trawler powered away, back to the harbour near Stavanger from where it had set sail the previous day, and sent off the message that was to shock the world.

'This is Northern Petroleum oil rig Alpha Bravo Discovery,' he read in his lightly accented English. 'It is now under the control of the Mourning Party. Over.'

In Aberdeen, the radio operator at NP headquarters heard but at first didn't believe the message. 'If this is a joke, Tom,' he said, thinking he was speaking to the rig boss, Tom Fowler, 'it's not funny. Over.'

'This is no joke,' said Jost. 'Now pay attention. My name is Eric Jost, and I am well known to your government. I have control of the rig, and certain demands which I do not intend to tell *you*. Get someone of authority in your organization to talk to me. I will call back in exactly five minutes. Over and out.' And he cut the connection.

The radio operator immediately called his supervisor, and as the operator vainly tried to restore radio communication, the supervisor phoned the headquarters chief. His name was Jim Conroy, and right away he called his head of security, Mike Anderson, and together they went to the radio room.

Precisely five minutes after he had aborted his first transmission, Eric Jost came back on the radio, and with a gesture from the supervisor, the radio operator put the message through the loudspeaker mounted on the wall in front of him.

'Oil rig Alpha Bravo Discovery to Northern Petroleum,' said Jost. 'Are you receiving? Over.'

Conroy took the mike and said: 'NP to Alpha Bravo Discovery. Receiving you loud and clear on strength ten. Jim Conroy speaking. Who are you? Over.'

'My name is Eric Jost, Mr Conroy. J-O-S-T. Are you a senior member of staff? Over.'

'I run this place, if that's what you mean. Over.'

'It's precisely what I mean. Now listen carefully to what I am about to say. Perhaps you should record this. Over.'

The supervisor had already switched on the cassette machine attached to the radio rig.

'It's done,' said Conroy. 'Over.'

'Good. Then I hope I won't have to repeat myself. As of ten hundred hours plus thirty this morning, your oil platform has been under the control of myself and my associates. It will remain under our control until you comply with certain demands.'

'Look,' interrupted Conroy. 'Is this a gag? I

don't mean to pour cold water on your little scheme. But you could be anyone calling from anywhere. Over.'

'Wait one. Over,' said Jost, and sent Bernais to fetch Tom Fowler from where he was being held at gunpoint in the control room.

When the rig boss was brought to the radio room, Jost put him on the air. 'Fowler to NP. Over,' he said.

'Who's that?' demanded Conroy. 'Over.'

'Tom Fowler, Mr Conroy. Over.'

'What's going on, Tom? Over.'

'Christ knows. Except a bunch of armed men came on board forty minutes or so ago, and took control of the rig. They sent out a fake mayday signal, and we fell for it. They've shut down all work and the men are under guard.' He glanced over at Jost, who nodded. 'I've got two injured paramedics here, and they shot Jodie Richards. He's dead. Over.'

Jodie Richards was the one worker who had tried to stop the take-over. One of Jost's troops had shot him dead.

'Christ,' said Conroy, as Jost took the microphone from Fowler and had him sent back to the control room.

'Do you believe me now? Over,' the German demanded.

'Yes,' said Conroy. 'What do you want? Over.'

'Good. Perhaps now we can do business. Over.'

'What kind of business? Over.'

'A transfer of funds. From your organization to mine. Over.'

'How much? Over.'

'Ten million pounds in cash. Used notes that can't be traced. Two million each in sterling, US dollars, German marks, French francs and Japanese yen. Hard currencies. Over.'

'I don't have that sort of money here. Over.'

'Don't be stupid, Mr Conroy. I hardly expected that you would. I'm going off air now, and that will give you a chance to contact your head office in London. They probably won't have that sort of money either. It's hardly petty cash. Even for an organization such as yours. But they can get it quickly enough. Over.'

'By when? Over.'

'You're learning, Mr Conroy. By this time tomorrow.' He looked at his watch. 'Shall we say noon. No later. And we want free passage in the helicopter you've so kindly provided. Over.'

'And what happens if the money is not forthcoming? Over.'

Don't even think about it, Mr Conroy. We have – what? – fifty hostages here on the rig. You presumably want them back. Over.'

'Of course. Over.'

'Then get the money, or you'll get them back dead. I'll call again in an hour. Over and out.' And once again he severed the radio link.

Conroy headed back to his office, Anderson the security chief in tow, after telling the supervisor and radio operator to say not one word to anyone else about what was happening. Once inside, he poured them both stiff Scotches and said: 'What do you think?'

'I think you should call London right now.'

'I think you're right,' said Conroy, who slumped into his chair and reached for the phone.

He got through to his head office and was put through to the managing director's secretary.

'He's in a meeting,' she said primly. 'Then he's off to lunch with the PM.'

'They'll have a lot to talk about,' said Conroy. 'Get him out of the meeting.'

'I can't do that.'

'Do you want a job tomorrow?'

'Of course.'

'Then do it.'

'Why? What shall I tell him?'

'Tell him one of his oil rigs has gone missing. That should concentrate his attention.'

'Are you serious?'

'Never more so.'

'I'll put you on hold.'

The story of my life, he thought, as the sound of a Paul Simon tune filled his ears.

Within thirty seconds, the distinctive, plummy tones of his managing director, Sir Jeremy Lion, came on the line. 'What the hell is going on up there,' he demanded. 'Are you drunk?'

Conroy looked longingly at the whisky bottle before he said: 'No, sir.'

'Then what is it?'

Conroy filled him in.

'Is this a bad joke?' Sir Jeremy demanded.

'I don't think so.'

'But you don't know.'

'Not for sure. I haven't been to the rig. I only just got the message. But Tom Fowler sounded pretty convincing.'

'And this fellow called himself Eric Jost?'

'That's what he said. He even spelt it.'

'Who else knows?'

Conroy told him.

'Then keep a lid on it. I'll be back to you directly. Don't leave the phone.'

'No, sir,' said Conroy, as the receiver at the other end was slammed down.

But someone else *did* know. On the outskirts of Aberdeen, a sixteen-year-old radio freak had been monitoring the calls between the oil company offices in the town and the rigs offshore, as he did often.

When he heard the dialogue between, first, the radio op at NP, and then Conroy, to Jost on Alpha Bravo Discovery, he went straight downstairs from his bedroom, where his radio set

146

was kept, to his mother in the kitchen, and told her.

'Are you sure, son?' she asked.

'Course I am, maw. I've been listening to those guys for more than a year, and nothing like this's ever happened before.'

'You didn't get a play on the radio by mistake.'

'On that frequency? Be sensible.'

His mother thought about it for a second. 'Then let me call the local paper. There might be something in it for us.'

She straight away called the *Aberdeen Argus*, and from a lifetime of watching TV, knew to ask for the news desk.

'News. McConnell,' said a brusque voice when she was put through.

'Are you a reporter?'

'That's what it says on my passport.'

'My name's Flynn. Maggie Flynn. My son Darren has been picking up some strange messages on his radio.'

'What, from aliens?'

Gerry McConnell had been on the news desk of a provincial newspaper for so long that nothing surprised him.

'No,' said Maggie Flynn. 'Something from an oil rig.'

'Like what?'

'I'll put him on, and he'll tell you himself.'

She handed the phone to Darren and he explained.

Gerry McConnell made notes of everything he said. He may have been on the news desk of a provincial newspaper for too long, but he recognized a passport to Wapping when he saw one. If it was true.

'Are you telling me the truth, son?' he asked.

'Yes. Course I am.'

'Give me your number there.'

Darren did so.

'I'm going to hang up now, and phone you back to verify this number,' said McConnell. 'Then I'm coming down. Is there anything on the radio now?'

'I don't know. I'm downstairs with me mam.'

'Then go back up and listen.'

McConnell terminated the call and dialled the number that Darren had given him. Maggie answered. 'I'm on my way,' said McConnell. 'Don't speak to anyone else.'

But he didn't leave the office before he checked the telex for any incoming stories concerning the rigs. There were none.

Good, he thought, and smiled grimly to himself. This one's mine.

Back on the submarine, after he'd heard the news that the army helicopter had gone down, and as McGough rushed into the room and read the message too, Valin said: 'Christ. That's rough. What happens now?'

'What happens now,' replied the commander, 'is

that we submerge and make our best speed back to the oil platform. I'm sorry, Valin, but that means you come with us.'

'What? We're due to deliver Lady Vanessa back to London and collect the balance of our fee.'

'You'll forgive me if I have very little sympathy with your plight. There is a bunk ready for you in McGough's cabin next door. I suggest you go there, and stay there until this business is dealt with.'

'How long will that be?'

'As long as a piece of string, I suspect. Now go away and leave us alone to get on with it. McGough, give the order to submerge and head north-east. Back to the oilfield at full speed.'

Valin did as he was told, found the tiny cabin, dumped his guns and jacket, washed his face in the minuscule hand bowl bolted to the bulkhead, and went looking for O'Rourke, whom he found sitting with Angel and Spenser in a tiny ward room. As he'd finished cleaning himself up, he'd felt the submarine submerge and head off as fast as its powerful engines would drive it.

'Hi, Colonel,' said Angel as he entered the room. 'Coffee?'

Valin nodded, and Angel poured a cup from a machine next to the serving hatch. 'All the comforts of home,' said the American when he brought the cup over. 'What's happening?'

Valin explained, and the other three men's faces fell at the news.

'Shit,' said Spenser. 'I'm pissed off with this thing already. I get claustrophobic, and this tin can's giving me the creeps.'

'Relax,' said O'Rourke. 'You're with the Royal Navy now. These things hardly ever sink.'

'Thanks, Mark,' said Spenser drily. 'I'll know who to come to next time I need some reassurance.'

'A pleasure. But, Colonel Valin, how long do you think this will take?'

'I know just what I've told you.'

'What's this Jost guy want?' asked Angel. 'And who is he?'

'Money, I imagine. What else do men like that ever work for? Once it was idealism, I imagine, but not any more. He was a big wheel in Baader-Meinhof in the seventies. But they splintered into a bunch of gangs of bank robbers in the end. A bit like us really. If I can collar McGough I'll get the full story. But I'm afraid our doughty commander doesn't like us very much. There wasn't as much as a word of congratulations when I saw him just now.'

'Maybe he knows how much we got paid,' said Angel with a grin. 'And he's got a hissy fit on about it.'

'Talking of pay,' said Valin. 'How is her ladyship?'

'She's got a hissy fit on too,' said Spenser. 'The mother of all moods in fact. Carmen and Trudy are taking care of her up front. There was a cabin laid on just for her.'

'So who the hell's on this boat?' said Angel. 'I've hardly seen a soul both times we've been on it.'

'Skeleton crew, I imagine,' said Valin. 'They don't want too many people knowing what we're up to. Careless talk and all that rot.'

'So what the hell's it supposed to do when it gets to the rig?'

'Christ knows,' replied Valin. 'But I'm sure it's going to be a memorable trip.'

And little did he know how right he was.

Sir Jeremy Lion was back on the telephone to Conroy at NP headquarters in Aberdeen within ten minutes. 'I've spoken to the Prime Minister,' the MD said. 'He's most perturbed.'

'I'm pleased to hear it,' replied Conroy drily. By that time he realized that nothing he said would put him in a good light, being the messenger of bad fortune. He knew too that sooner or later a scapegoat would have to be found for the whole mess, and that it was quite possible that his name would head the list. So he might as well say what he thought, and at least go out with some dignity left. And, as he was the man on the spot, and had the best local knowledge, at least until the rig was liberated, he was a very necessary player in the game that had started that morning. 'And what does he intend doing about it?'

'He's contacted the army Chief of Staff, and they're going to rush a platoon of commandos from Northern Ireland by helicopter to the rig and recapture it.'

'As simple as that,' said Conroy. 'Believe me, sir . . .' – he almost balked at the word – 'it's not going to be easy. Jost's men have hostages, and a lot of expensive equipment on that platform. Plus, I'm sure they have the means to destroy it easily. Even if they didn't take any explosives with them, which I doubt, they won't have to look far to find some volatile material on board. And the weather is appalling up here. And in the final analysis, how easy will it be for the troops to get on to the site without being blown out of the air?'

'One of Her Majesty's submarines, which happened to be in the area on another mission, is, even as we speak, checking out the area,' replied the MD. 'They will come back to the Admiralty with the latest intelligence within the hour.'

'Fair enough. And talking about the hour. What about the money? Jost is going to call back in about thirty minutes. What do I tell him?'

'Stall him.'

'Don't be stupid.'

'What did you say?'

'You heard me, sir. I meant no offence. May I just suggest that as Plan B, so to speak, someone should gather together the ten million. Just in case everything goes pear-shaped up here.'

Sir Jeremy was silent for a moment. 'Very well,' he said. 'Perhaps you're right. It can't do any harm, I suppose. But it's a damn nuisance.' And he slammed down the phone.

'Probably make him miss his lunch,' said Anderson. 'Too fucking bad.'

'Maybe he'll send out for a sandwich,' said Conroy.

'I hope it gives the bastard indigestion.'

So, while the battle for Lochnercrag was being fought by Valin's team, the submarine had been sent from its position just off the island, out to the rig, and so many messages had been flashing between the ship and London, that Willis's calls had not been answered.

Meanwhile, at an army airfield near Belfast, a platoon of élite commandos had been mustered, issued with cold-weather gear, extra ammunition, and life-jackets, and hurriedly loaded on to a Bell/Boeing V-22 Osprey twin-turbo helicopter, and were waiting for the command from Whitehall to leave for the rig.

The order came at fourteen hundred hours, and the helicopter clawed its way up into the worsening weather, and set off on a north-easterly course.

It should have been a routine flight. The chopper was fitted with the latest state-of-the-art navigational equipment. But something went badly wrong after they cleared the east coast of Scotland and were heading for the rig. Sometime around sixteen hundred hours, contact was lost with the chopper, and a crofter on a lonely island saw a flash of light on the tor that dominated it, closely followed by an explosion, and after a long climb to the top of the peak found the burnt-out debris of the aircraft scattered down the side of a huge outcrop of rock, and the dead bodies of its passengers. There were no survivors. The black box flight recorder was never recovered, and to this day no one has been able to ascertain the exact cause of the tragedy.

The news was relayed by radio to the mainland, and eventually to the submarine that was carrying Valin and his cohorts, and fresh orders were given for it to head back to the rig.

That lunchtime, Conroy had begun his attempt to stall Jost about the ransom money. The German's call had come in, precisely as he'd promised, an hour after he'd terminated their previous conversation. 'Platform Alpha Bravo Discovery to NP. Come in. Over.'

'NP to Alpha Bravo Discovery. Reading you loud and clear, over,' said Conroy.

'Mr Conroy. Eric Jost here. What is your state of play? Over.'

'I have contacted my superiors in London. They have agreed to your terms, and the money is being raised. However, you must appreciate that, even for a company of our size, such a sum is to say the least unusual. Especially in the mixed currencies you stipulated. And it will take some time to put it together. Over.'

'I'm glad that your lords and masters have been clear-headed enough to realize that to refuse would end in tragedy. You have my time limit. Noon tomorrow. What about the passage for our chopper? Over.'

'As you requested. Clean and green. Over.' Conroy lied.

'Very good. Listen on this frequency. I may call again. Over and out.'

And Conroy, Anderson and the radio operator were left listening to dead air.

In Darren's tiny, stuffy, untidy bedroom in the block of flats on the edge of Aberdeen, he and McConnell also heard the dialogue. McConnell recorded the message on his micro-recorder and turned to Darren with a smile. 'You were right, son,' he said triumphantly.

'What did I tell you?' said the boy. 'I knew something was wrong as soon as I heard the first message.'

'And I'm glad you came straight to me,' said McConnell. 'You and your mum won't lose financially by it, I promise. Now I'll need to use your phone.'

The news broke in the late-afternoon edition of the paper, pushing to page two a fire at a tyre factory that had taken the life of two workers and

a fireman. In banner headlines, the story began:
OIL RIG HIJACKED – £10 MILLION RANSOM
DEMANDED. The piece went on to give the bare
facts as McConnell knew them from Darren, and a
'no comment' quote from NP House in London.

Conroy and his managing director found out that
the story had broken at precisely the same time,
when newsflashes interrupted the programmes on
the TV sets that they both had on in their offices.

The MD, who by this time had had a conference
line system set up between his office, Conroy's,
Downing Street and the Ministry of Defence in
Whitehall, cursed like the old soldier he was. 'How
the hell did it get out, Conroy?' he barked into
the phone.

'I have no idea, sir. Not from here at least. The
radio room's phone has been disconnected, and
Anderson and I have been together ever since the
first communication.'

'Perhaps you have a big-eared friend listening
in,' put in the languid voice of the man from the
MoD. 'I've just had a copy of the paper faxed down
from Aberdeen. The byline is in the name of Gerald
McConnell. I'm having Special Branch pay him a
visit. More later.'

McConnell was picked up from his office within
five minutes, and taken to the local police station
to wait for Special Branch to arrive from Glasgow.
It turned out to be a long wait, but McConnell

had already sold Darren's name and address to a London daily newspaper in exchange for a job on its news desk, which was what he'd always wanted.

15

As the afternoon darkened into evening, a strange calm permeated the oil rig. The snow was thick, and lay on every flat surface, but the weather kept away the fleets of media aircraft and boats that would otherwise have been circling the platform on the sea and in the air, so the only sound was the wind and the sea.

Jost and Bernais were in the radio shack drinking coffee, smoking cigarettes, and monitoring the radio waves, while the rest of the men kept the crew confined to the mini-cinema, two floors below.

They picked up none of the Admiralty's messages to the sub, as they were sent by microwave direct from a satellite above Birmingham, but they did get the local and national radio stations that were carrying the news, and frantically trying to get in touch with Alpha Bravo Discovery for some news from the horse's mouth.

Jost let them wait.

'You think they'll come across with the cash?' asked the Frenchman.

'Not if they can help it. I'm expecting some kind of visit any time now,' replied Jost, not realizing that just about then, the Bell/Boeing helicopter carrying twenty-four troops and its crew of three was smashing to the ground, only a few miles away from where they sat.

'Bastards,' said Bernais, as Jost monitored the radar for any sign of an approaching vessel or plane.

'What did you expect, Pierre? That they'd give in without a fight? We have made the government of Great Britain, and one of its largest companies, a laughing-stock. I think we're lucky to be sitting where we are, without rockets being aimed at our arses.'

Bernais laughed. 'I don't think so, Eric. This place is too valuable to blow away.'

'Maybe. But I'm sure we'll have someone breathing down our necks before long. Now, I might just call up NP and see how they're going.'

'I'm sure they'll be glad to hear from you.'

'A little dig with a pointed stick never did a pig any harm, and just got him home all the quicker,' Jost said with a thin smile, and reached for the microphone.

'Alpha Bravo Discovery to NP. Over,' he intoned, and had a feeling that a thousand pairs of ears were listening to his voice.

'NP to Alpha Bravo Discovery,' came the reply from Conroy, who had moved his office, complete with conference line, down to the radio room. 'Receiving you strength ten. Come in, over.'

'Mr Conroy, I have been thinking,' said Jost. 'Over.'

'Yes. Over,' said Conroy, his heart sinking. What the hell did the man want now?

'I feel we have made some ripples in the international pool,' said the German. 'And it occurs to me that your government might want to get involved.'

Conroy thought of the chopper, still unaware of the crash.

'I have no knowledge of that,' he said, lying for the second time.

'Well, if they do, be kind enough to explain that if I see any sign of aggression whatsoever towards us or the platform, it will be my unwelcome task to execute ten of the workers. Over.'

Conroy's heart sunk even further.

'I'm sure there will be no moves made against you, Mr Jost. Over,' he said.

'But just to make the situation plain. I'm sure that you won't have to spread the news. I imagine every word is being monitored. Over.'

'I don't know about that,' said Conroy. 'Over.'

'Whatever. Keep listening. And remember, time is passing. Over and out.'

The news made the evening bulletins. A government spokesman spouted a platitude-filled speech, and a spokeswoman for NP did the same.

Meanwhile the news was spreading about the chopper crash, and Valin and his soldiers of fortune were about to get into the game.

The submarine was speeding through the cold, grey waters of the North Sea, and everyone who had come off the island of Lochnercrag apart from Lady Vanessa, who was locked in her cabin with a burly naval MP in front of it, had gathered in the mess hall at Valin's behest. He explained the situation and waited for comments.

'Typical,' said Angel. 'Another run-around.'

Valin shrugged and said: 'What the hell can we do? We're stuck in this thing and we've just got to be patient.'

'OK, Colonel,' said the American. 'I guess we're stuck with the short end again. Anyone got a deck of cards?'

Just as he was speaking, a coded message came through to the conning tower of the submarine. It was from Sir Hadley Bryant-Marshall, who had already received confirmation that the mission to Lochnercrag had been a success, and a list of the survivors. It was to the commander of the submarine, and read:

Weather too bad to contemplate sending more troops from Northern Ireland. You only vessel in vicinity. Use your available personnel plus

Colonel Valin and his men to storm NP oil rig Alpha Bravo Discovery. Liaise with Captain Willis in first instance. Please confirm. Bryant-Marshall.

'Christ,' said the commander to McGough. 'Whose bloody bright idea was this?'

'Needs must,' said the lieutenant.

'When the bloody devil drives, is right,' said the commander. 'And which one is this Willis character?'

'He's a professional soldier,' explained McGough, 'the one with his arm in a sling.' 'Seconded in with his mate McCall. And neither of them is too happy about it as far as I can gather.'

'I can't say I blame them. Who the hell have we got on board that can manage this sort of job?'

'The two MPs should be up to it. Bryers and Smith. And there's always me. I've been up for special weapons training.'

'So you have. That makes how many?'

'Ten.'

'Right. Where's this Willis?'

'In the mess hall with the rest of them.'

'Well, wheel the bugger in. And be discreet, for Christ's sake, John. Just tell him we've got a message for him. OK?'

McGough saluted, did an about turn and headed for the mess hall.

When he walked in he spotted Willis and went up to him. 'You've got a message from London,' he said.

'Is that right?'

'Yes.'

'So where is it?'

'The commander's got it. He needs a word.'

'About what?' Valin had overheard.

'Don't know, sir. I haven't seen it,' lied McGough.

'More good news, I expect,' said Angel.

'Well, go on then, Willis, double up,' said Valin. 'And maybe we'll all be the wiser.'

Willis accompanied McGough to the conning tower, where the commander handed him the message slip.

'Christ almighty,' said Willis, when he'd read it twice. 'How many other men do you have who could do this sort of job?'

The commander told him.

'Wonderful,' said Willis, looking at McGough.

'Happy?' said the commander.

'No,' was Willis's reply. 'Can I answer it?'

'Be my guest,' said the commander. 'But I don't think you're going to have much joy.'

Willis worded a message of his own to London: 'Strongly suggest that using Valin's troops for this job a mistake. Please reconsider. Willis.'

The answer wasn't long in coming. It was short and to the point: 'Consider previous message an order. No time to waste. Bryant-Marshall.'

'Shit,' said Willis. 'I guess I've got no choice. I'd better have a word with Valin.'

'Good luck,' said the commander, and Willis went back to the mess hall.

'A word, Colonel,' he said.

'Of course.'

'In private if we may.'

'My cabin is just down the companion-way.'

When they were in the tiny cabin, with the door shut, Willis showed Valin the first message. He didn't mention his reply, and the subsequent order.

Valin shook his head and handed the thin piece of paper back to the young captain. 'Forget it,' he said.

'I rather thought you might say that.'

'What did you expect? We were hired to do a job, which we've done, and lost three men as a result. Now Bryant-Marshall wants us to do another. Up against Christ knows how many desperate men. We've got walking wounded. How many was the commander prepared to put in the pot?'

'Three,' Willis said, and told him who.

'Outstanding. But we don't have to do anything we don't want to. And I see there's no mention of money.'

'No, sir.'

'Then get back on to London and tell Bryant-Marshall that I refuse. Thanks, but no thanks.'

'Yes, sir,' said Willis with relief.

He left the colonel and went back to the conning tower. 'No go,' he said to the commander. 'Valin refused point-blank. Can I send another message?'

'Of course.'

This time it read: 'Valin says no. One job is enough for one day. I await further orders. Willis.'

'They're going to love that,' said the commander as he handed the slip to the radio operator. 'I can just see their faces now.'

The reply arrived a few minutes later: 'Offer Valin one million sterling to reconsider. If he still refuses, arrest him and his group for murder. Bryant-Marshall.'

'Rather you than me,' said the commander. 'I think you'll probably need some backup.'

Valin was back in the mess hall when Willis went looking for him again, this time with the two MPs in tow. Both policemen were wearing holstered Colt automatics, and carried machine-pistols at port arms. 'Another word, Colonel,' Willis said.

'Of course.'

'Shall we go to your cabin?'

'No. You can speak to me here. We have no secrets. The rest are aware of what's going on. And what's with your friends?'

'Just a precaution.'

McCall, who had been sitting alone at one of the tables, stood up.

'A precaution?' said Valin. 'Or is it coercion?'

'I hope it won't come to that, Colonel.'

'Speak your piece, then.'

'I've been authorized to offer you a million pounds sterling to capture the rig.'

'Another million,' said Valin. 'The British taxpayer is going to feel the pinch.'

'It's a serious matter.'

'Of course it is. And what's the alternative?'

'Not a nice one, I'm afraid. Bryant-Marshall has given me orders to arrest you if you refuse.'

'On what charge?'

'Murder.'

Valin smiled mirthlessly. 'Well, I don't know,' he said. 'I shall have to speak to my troops.'

'I'll give you five minutes. McCall, come with me, and leave these people to make up their minds. I would, however, ask you to let me take any weapons you're carrying.'

The two MPs swung their guns down to cover the group.

Valin raised his hands in a gesture of surrender. 'I don't really think any of us want loose bullets puncturing the hull of this vessel,' he said, looking round. 'Hand over any firearms, ladies and gentlemen. I think we have a *fait accompli* here.'

Reluctantly, Angel took out the Colt .45 he was wearing, and put it on the table for McCall to collect. Spenser was the only other armed man in Valin's team, and after a moment's thought he handed over his Browning.

'Do I have to have everyone searched?' asked Willis. 'Or can I take your word as an officer and a gentleman that this is the sum total of your ordnance?'

'You can take my word or not, as you please,' said Valin. 'But I trust my men. You'll have no trouble from any of us.'

Willis nodded stiffly, and he, McCall and the two MP's left the mess hall.

'Fucking hell,' said Angel. 'Another fine mess we've got ourselves into.'

'I'm glad you're not blaming me,' said Valin.

'It's hardly your fault, Colonel,' said O'Rourke.

'Listen, man, I'm only blaming myself for being stuck in this tin can, with all the cash back in London town,' said Angel. 'So what do you say, Colonel?'

'More to the point, what do you say?' Valin replied.

'A cut of another million. Sounds cool to me,' said Angel.

'Chris?' asked the colonel.

'I could do with having the first lot, then deciding what I do with the rest of my life,' said Spenser.

'It might be in some high-security prison,' said O'Rourke. 'If they carry out their threats.'

'I think they're bluffing,' said Valin. 'But I wouldn't put it past Bryant-Marshall to disappear us off the face of the earth.'

'What does that mean?' asked Trudy, who

had been sitting in a corner, listening intently.

Valin made a throat-cutting gesture with his forefinger.

'Kill us?' she said.

'Think of all the money it would save them,' said the colonel. 'So what does everyone say?'

'We could do the job and they just disappear us anyway,' put in Carmen.

'Not if we're smart,' said her husband. 'And they've got to give us our guns back. And us with a bunch of automatic weapons are more than a match for anyone the British can throw at us.'

'I'm amazed you have so little faith in our armed services,' said Valin.

'You know me, Colonel,' said Spenser. 'I *never* look on the bright side unless I've got a gun in my hand.'

'Try one of these for size, then,' said Angel, and produced two more Brownings from under his jacket. 'Sorry, Colonel, but no one ever accused me of being either an officer *or* a gentleman.'

'I might've guessed,' said Valin. 'But before we resort to force, let's take a vote. Who goes for it?'

O'Rourke and Angel raised raised their hands right away. Spenser and Carmen looked at each other. 'Oh hell,' said Spenser. 'Why not?' And he raised his hand too, closely followed by Carmen.

'Unanimous,' said Valin, finally raising his own hand. 'Put away the guns, Angel. But everyone, stay on the ball. The stakes are getting higher, and I think we might have a couple of jokers in the pack.'

* * *

Exactly five minutes to the second after they'd left the mess hall, Willis, McCall and the two MPs returned, this time bringing McGough with them. McCall was carrying his Browning in his hand, its hammer cocked. 'Have you come to a decision?' asked Willis.

'Yes, we have,' replied Valin. 'You win. We go.'

'Good,' said Willis. 'And no tricks, I hope.'

'An officer and a gentleman,' said Valin.

McCall returned his gun to its holster, and the five newcomers sat down at a table with Valin. 'Bryers and Smith,' said Willis, introducing the two MPs. 'The lieutenant you know. That makes us ten-handed. Is that sufficient?'

'Sufficient to get us all killed,' said Angel.

'First things first,' said Valin. 'We need confirmation that the money will be waiting when we get back. *If* we get back. I hate to be mercenary, but that's the name of the game.'

'I'll contact London as soon as we're done here,' said Willis. 'Don't worry, you'll get your money.'

'I know we will,' said Valin. 'Now when do we get to this confounded oil rig?'

'In about forty minutes,' said McGough. 'It gives us just time to come up with a plan.'

'The plan is to get on, kill anything that moves,

and get off as soon as possible,' said Valin. 'Isn't that right?'

'Not quite,' said Willis. 'There is the matter of the fifty-odd crew members to consider. We have to take their safety into consideration.'

'Are they taking ours?' asked Angel.

'Probably not. But they are civilians. The majority of them are British subjects, and their safety is paramount.'

'And ours isn't,' Angel said wryly.

'We are expendable.'

'Speak for yourself,' Angel hissed.

'Are you taking control of this mission? asked Valin coolly.

'I think I should, sir,' said Willis. 'Don't you?'

'I don't take orders from anyone but the colonel,' said Angel firmly.

'Me neither,' said Spenser.

Carmen nodded her agreement with the two men.

'Or me,' added O'Rourke.

Willis considered. 'Very well,' he said. 'Colonel Valin is in charge. I bow to his authority.'

'And the rest of you?' Valin said.

After a moment, McCall, McGough and the two MPs nodded their assent.

'Thank you,' said Valin. 'Now I don't suppose we have a plan of this place.'

'One is being sent by satellite,' said Willis. 'It should be here by now.'

'Will you fetch it then?' said Valin. 'And don't forget the message about our money. One million in old notes. Not consecutive serial numbers. You never know who to trust these days.'

'Of course, sir,' said Willis, his voice heavy with sarcasm.

'You'll get used to us,' said Valin. 'It's early days yet.'

Willis took McGough and McCall with him, leaving the MPs in the mess hall. The plan of the rig was waiting for him, and he sent the required message to Bryant-Marshall about the money, and got an affirmative reply.

Shit, he thought, thinking of his own monthly pay cheque. Maybe there is something to be said for this mercenary lark after all.

'I'll get this blueprint to Valin and tell him and the rest the good news about the money,' he said to the commander. 'McCall, come with me.'

'Sir,' said McCall, and with twin salutes to the commander, they left the bridge.

A few minutes later, the radar officer said to the commander: 'We're two miles from the rig, sir. I've engaged the Stealth Mechanism. With the weather topside, they won't be able to pick us up on their radar.' The Stealth Mechanism was a new, computer-enhanced apparatus, derived from the plane of the same name, which made any object virtually invisible to radar.

'Good man,' said the commander. 'Let's take a look.' And he ordered the submarine to be brought up to periscope level.

But it was impossible. When the periscope was up, all he could see through the darkness was the snow drifting down on to the sea.

'Pointless,' he exclaimed to McGough, bringing down the 'scope. 'You're going to have to go in by the seat of your pants.'

He turned to the lieutenant, who was standing next to him, his face eerie in the reflection from the radar screen. 'Have you requisitioned your weapons?'

'Sir,' said McGough.

'Take two inflatables. And keep in close contact. I want to know if we have to come in to pick up the crew. Or you lot for that matter.'

'If any of us make it,' said McGough.

'You will.'

'I wish I had your faith, commander. This whole thing is half-arsed, to say the least.'

'So was Trafalgar.'

'I hope we do half as well as Lord Nelson,' said McGough drily.

'So do I,' replied the commander.

'How close are you going to get?'

'Another mile, I think. Then we'll go up, and you can shove off.'

'I'll inform the others,' said McGough.

'Do that. And good luck.'

'Thank you, sir,' said McGough, then saluted and left.

Everyone else was waiting in the mess hall, and after Willis's news that the cash was forthcoming, they had all been allowed to collect their weapons, and their cold-weather gear.

'We go in about twenty minutes,' said McGough to Valin, who was busy looking over the plan of the platform. 'We're taking the two inflatables to the rig.'

'Have we been spotted?' asked the colonel.

'No. We've got a radar-fooling gizmo in operation. The screen on the platform should show clean and green.'

'Thank Christ for that anyway,' said Angel, checking the magazine in his Scorpion. 'At least there won't be a welcoming committee.'

16

In London, phones and faxes were buzzing busily, as news of the hijack was made public through special editions of the evening papers and TV newsflashes, and various government departments were getting involved in the crisis.

Sir Hadley Bryant-Marshall was at the eye of the hurricane, and his Whitehall office had become the nerve centre of the operation to recapture Alpha Bravo Discovery. On his desk was an open line to Downing Street, another to the boardroom of NP's London headquarters, and a third to Conroy, at the company's Aberdeen offices.

As the blizzard reached London, at the same time as Valin and his squad were preparing to disembark from the submarine for the perilous journey to the platform, Bryant-Marshall was talking to the Prime Minister.

'It's our only option, sir,' he said. 'There is no chance of getting anything else up there until tomorrow afternoon at the earliest. We just don't have a ship of the line in the vicinity that can do it. The weather's just too bad. And Jost's deadline is noon. And I know from old that he means it.'

'What are the instructions for delivering the money?' came the measured tones of the PM.

'None as yet. Jost's too seasoned a veteran to give anything away until the last moment. Is the money being organized?'

'Yes. Sir Jeremy is personally supervising it. But he, like me, wants to know how anything like this could be allowed to happen. What went wrong, Hadley? How was it allowed to get this far? Have we no intelligence working on these terrorist gangs? People will be asking questions, and you know there's an election looming.'

'It's been our nightmare for years,' replied Bryant-Marshall. 'This and every previous administration. We've all known it could happen, but we've just prayed that it never would. Of course we try and keep tabs on these people, and what they're up to. But you know what they're like, as well as I do. Will-o'-the-Wisp has nothing on some of these characters. They travel the world as if they own it, financed by every lunatic government and organization under the sun. The FO budget just doesn't stretch to having them under surveillance on a permanent basis. What could we do, save have a destroyer anchored off every oil rig in the North Sea, twenty-four hours a day?'

The Prime Minister ignored the question. 'And he has a helicopter on the platform?'

'Yes, sir. A twelve-seater Sikorsky is ready to go. And a pilot, if he doesn't have one of his own.'

'How does he propose to use it if the weather's as bad as I've heard it is?'

'Some people have no concern for their own safety,' said Bryant-Marshall matter-of-factly. 'After all, it was a pretty risky venture in the first place, stealing something that size. I mean, sir, it's pretty hard to hide.'

There was a long pause, and Bryant-Marshall wondered if he'd overstepped the mark, as he watched the snowflakes flutter down past his window, each one momentarily spotlighted by the light from inside his warm office.

'I don't like it, Hadley,' said the PM. 'Sending these bloody cowboys into war for us. That picnic on Lochnercrag was one thing, but this is another. These people will be able to name their own price to the newspapers worldwide if they succeed. No: if they only survive. Can you imagine it?'

'I can, sir.'

'So what are you proposing to do about it?'

'I have two men of my own with them, as you know. They're both good. They've both done more for their country in their time than could reasonably be expected. I've sent another message to Willis telling him what happens at the end of the exercise, win or lose.'

'Do I want to hear this, Hadley?' asked the PM cautiously.

'You did ask, sir.'

Another pause. 'Very well. Continue.'

'Whatever happens, none of Valin's men, or the woman for that matter, must be allowed to get back to the mainland. As soon as they stepped on to that submarine this morning, to all intents and purposes they signed their own death warrants.'

'Isn't this getting rather machiavellian?'

'Machiavelli was a very fine politician, sir.'

'I suppose you're right.'

'I know I am, sir.'

'This is a nightmare, Hadley. Since the damn media got hold of the story, it's been like a madhouse down here. You can't move outside for reporters and camera crews, even in this bloody weather.'

'I'm not surprised. But at least be thankful for the weather up *there*. Everything's grounded for hundreds of miles, and no nosy cameraman can get out to the rig. At least we'll have no witnesses.'

'I heard that a reporter from the *Sun* was offering £50,000 to any chopper pilot who was prepared to take him out to the site.'

'So did I. Thank goodness no one took up the offer. If anyone had, he'd have been blown out of the air by a heat-seeking missile from the sub.'

'Aren't we getting rather above ourselves here?'

'Not at all, sir. Sometimes the end justifies the means.'

'Isn't that what Hitler said?'

'Probably – but then he wasn't such a bad politician either.'

Willis decoded the final message in the cabin he'd been designated, while he waited for McGough to oversee the preparation of the inflatables. He pulled a wry face to himself before destroying the message slip, then went looking for McCall.

'I've had a shout from the boss,' he said, when he'd pulled his partner away from the others.

'Yeah?' said McCall.

'Yeah. Bad news, I'm afraid. Whatever happens, none of our friends make it back home.'

'Are you joking?'

'No.'

'Well, that's unfortunate for them. But they're no pushover. Can we use the sailors?'

'If we have to.'

'We'd better. I don't want any witnesses who didn't take part in the deed.'

'They're professional servicemen.'

'So?'

'So they do as they're told.'

'Do you really think they're up to it?'

'They're trained,' said Willis.

'Not in assassination.'

'So?'

'So if they don't help us, they're bloody dead themselves.'

'You're a cold-blooded bastard, Jason.'

'I've always been noted for it. But it's kept me alive so far.'

'I hope *I* never have to watch my back when you're around.'

'The feeling's mutual, Captain Willis.'

Willis allowed himself a rare smile. 'Then we'll just have to watch each other's, won't we?'

And so the final part of the mercenaries' mission began. Thirty minutes after their final briefing, they heard the klaxons howl as the submarine surfaced, and McGough and Willis oversaw the launching once again of the two inflatables, their bright-orange rubber skins made the colour of the sea with camouflage paint.

The submarine was tossed from wave top to wave top by the fierce seas as everyone lent a hand in getting the small vessels on deck and into the water. Finally, they were afloat, and the ten bodies piled into them, five in each boat. McGough took the tiller of one, Valin of the other, and joined by a thin nylon rope, they turned in the direction of the oil rig.

Back in London, Bryant-Marshall was sitting in his leather swivel chair, thinking about his final message to Willis.

I hope the boy knows what he's letting himself in for, he reflected, as his secretary brought him in a cup of coffee, and poured a cognac from the decanter on the filing cabinet disguised as a sideboard. I really do.

Then the phone rang again. It was the direct line from the Prime Minister. Bryant-Marshall winced as he picked up the receiver. What now? he thought, as he dismissed the woman with a wave of his hand.

'Hadley,' said the PM.

'Sir?'

'I've been talking to Jeremy at NP. He's worried about sending this crew on to his rig. Or more precisely, his shareholders' rig.'

'He's not the only one, if I may say so, sir. Only some of us are more concerned about the men involved, rather than the shareholders.'

'Be that as it may. We have to make sure, in writing, that your men out there realize the full implications of what's happening here.'

'I'm sure they do, sir.'

'And I want you to know that I'm holding you personally responsible for that rig, and every crew member on board.'

'I expected nothing less.'

'So you'll be sure to send them a message to that effect?'

'Of course, sir.'

'We'll speak later, then. And no matter what time it is, be sure to notify me of any development.'

'Of course, sir.'

'Until we speak again, then.' With that, the Prime Minister put down the phone.

Bryant-Marshall looked at the dead instrument in his hand before he carefully replaced it on its stand.

The buck stops here, he thought, and reached for a message pad. He looked at it for a moment, before smiling grimly and pushing it away.

It would have been too late anyway. Even as Bryant-Marshall was sipping at his cognac, and looking at the blank message sheet, Valin, his men, Carmen, Willis, McCall and the three sailors were pounding their way through the icy seas towards the oil rig and the battle of their lives.

17

The inflatables passed between the massive metal struts that anchored the rig to the seabed, the sound of their engines lost in the crying of the wind that tore across Europe straight from the Urals. Up in the control room, Jost was looking at the radar screen, which, confusingly, was jumping with secondary echoes from the snowstorm. 'Christ,' he said to Bernais. 'This weather's fucking up the reception. I'm sure there's something down there, but I can't be certain.'

'Want me to take a look?'

'If you can see anything in this muck.'

'I'll try.'

'Go on, then. But be careful. Get one of the other guys to back you up.'

'Sure,' said the Frenchman, as he zipped up his jacket, grabbed his machine-pistol and went outside into the vile weather. He thought about finding another of the terrorists to watch his back, but thought again, shrugged, and decided to do it alone. It would be too much trouble to go down to the cinema where they were keeping the platform workers prisoner and dig one out. After all, Bernais had been able to look after himself for years. Why should this day prove to be any different?

He delicately negotiated the slippery walkway to the edge of the platform, slung his gun round his shoulder, knocked snow off the balustrade and peered down through the murk. He could see nothing, because the inflatables were already tied up to one of the landing-stages at the bottom of a steep flight of icy steps, and their colours merged with the grey sea.

He decided to get a closer look. Years of being on the wrong side of the law had honed his instinct for self-preservation to a razor edge, and he had a gut feeling that something was definitely up.

As Bernais began to descend the stairs, at the bottom Valin tapped Angel on the shoulder and said in his ear. 'Go up. See if they've posted a guard. And for Christ's sake try not to be seen. We'll be sitting ducks down here if anyone spots us.'

Angel nodded, and swung himself up over the edge of the landing-stage, and with his bare fingers already freezing in the cold, started up towards the platform that loomed darkly above him.

Carefully, Bernais picked his way down, the wind whipping at his clothes, until he was close enough to sea level to feel the spray from the waves that beat against the legs of the platform.

When he was as far down as he dared go, he made a circle with his hands to shield his eyes, and looked out to sea, gradually turning through 360 degrees as he did so. When he had almost returned to his original position he felt the freezing metal of a gun barrel on the unprotected skin behind his right ear, and a lazy American voice whispered: 'Take it easy, big boy, or I'll blow your head off.'

Bernais responded by ducking down low, kicking back with one heel, and trying to bring his gun up to a firing position, but Angel was prepared for the manoeuvre, and slammed the barrel of his Colt .45 down on his head as hard as he could, twice. The blows left the Frenchman groggy but still conscious, and Angel hissed: 'I warned you, you bastard. Will you listen or do you want to get dead?'

The terrorist leant against the thin railing that was the only thing between him and the sea below and groaned: 'OK, OK, you win.'

'I know that,' said Angel. 'It was only you that wasn't convinced.'

The rest of the force from the sub, who had seen what was happening above them, swarmed up the ladder, and the naval MP pulled the Frenchman's hands up behind his back and secured them with one of the pairs of plastic handcuffs he'd brought with him.

'One down,' said Valin. 'I wonder how many that leaves to go?'

'Tell us, big boy,' said Angel, pulling Bernais round on the step. 'Or shall I throw you into the sea, and give the fishes an early dinner?'

Bernais spat in his face and Angel hit him on the point of the jaw with his gun. The terrorist fell back against the railing, and Angel raised his pistol again.

'Leave him,' hissed Valin. 'He's more use to us alive than dead.'

'But it'd be such a pleasure to blow him away.'

Valin turned to Bernais. 'How many more of you are there?' he asked.

'Find out.'

'Do you want me to give you back to my colleague? I'm sure he'd have fun making you talk.'

'He could try.'

'And succeed probably. But it would waste precious time.'

Valin turned to the MP. 'Disarm him, and secure him to the railings,' he said. 'We'll leave him here for now.'

'I'll freeze,' protested Bernais.

'Too bad,' said Valin. The Frenchman already forgotten, he squinted up through the metalwork at the platform and said: 'No one else seems very interested. I think he was on his own.'

'Wait,' said Bernais. 'I'll tell you what you want to know. Just don't leave me.'

The MP, who had relieved the terrorist of his machine-pistol and the Smith & Wesson revolver he was carrying on his hip, plus a flick-knife and set of brass knuckledusters, looked at Valin. The colonel nodded, and the MP put the Frenchman's own handgun to his head and said: 'Just don't fuck me around, boy. Or I'll finish the job.'

Bernais was thinking frantically about how to turn the tables, and let Jost, still up in the control room, know what was going on. 'I won't, monsieur,' he said in a wheedling tone. 'I don't want to die.'

Slowly, the party climbed the steps up to the platform.

'How many of you are there?' Valin repeated his question to the Frenchman as they went.

'Six in all, monsieur.'

'If you're lying . . .'

'As if I would,' he lied. 'I value my life too highly.'

'Where are they?'

'In the mess hall,' he lied again.

'With the crew?'

'*Oui.*'

'None on the outside?'

'*Non.* The weather is too bad. And we thought there was no danger of anyone coming aboard, not with the conditions as they are.'

'Especially when you threatened to murder ten men if they did.'

Bernais nodded.

'You were wrong then, weren't you?'

'How did you get here? We saw nothing on the radar.'

'Modern technology,' said Valin. 'It's amazing what they can do these days.'

The terrorist looked out to sea. 'Is there something out there?'

'You're fast,' said Angel. 'Did you graduate near the top of the class?'

'What about communications to the outside world?' asked Valin.

'One man is monitoring the radio.'

'And Jost?'

'With the rest in the mess hall.'

The Frenchman's mind was racing. There had to be a way to warn his comrades, and suddenly he saw one. They were passing the door to a storeroom. It was open, and inside on the wall was a panic button in case of emergency. Bernais thought this filled the bill, and as they passed the door, he lunged away from the MP, threw himself into the room and rammed his shoulder against the button, which started klaxons screaming all over the rig.

'Bastard,' yelled Angel and cut him down with a burst of metal-jacketed bullets from his Scorpion. Bernais was knocked away from the button, but the alarms kept howling, and Valin and the rest knew that the game was up.

'Can't you stop the fucking thing,' said O'Rourke, 'it's giving me a headache,' as Angel and the MP vainly looked for some way to turn off the alarm.

Up in the radar room, Jost shot out of his seat as if he'd been given an electric shock, grabbed his rifle and went to the door. Outside, the alarms were even louder, coming and going as the wind caught the sound and hurled it out to sea.

He peered round, looking for the Frenchman, then dashed back into the radar room, out into the corridor that ran alongside it, and jogged in the direction of the staircase that led to the cinema on the lowest level, to be met by two of his men as they came out to see what was going on. 'Have you seen Pierre?' Jost shouted, before they could speak.

They shook their heads in tandem, and he said: 'Didn't he come to get one of you to help him outside?'

'No, boss,' said one of them, a Cypriot named Grima, who had worked as a wildcatter on oil rigs for many months, and had supplied a lot of the information that had made the hijacking of Alpha Bravo Discovery possible.

'Now come on, then, help me find him,' yelled Jost.

They all ran up to one of the exits to the platform. Outside it was pitch-black, the snow swirled around them like snakes and they could see nothing through the darkness. 'We need lights,' screamed Jost. 'And some way to turn that damn alarm off.'

As if by magic, the klaxons stopped, just as Grima hit a switch which illuminated the outside of the rig. 'I didn't waste my time on that platform,' he said proudly, as a bullet shattered the window he was standing in front of, tore through his chest and knocked him to the metal floor, his gun clattering after him.

'Christ,' said Jost as he and the other man, an American by the name of Sinclair, hit the deck too. 'The bastards have already got on board.'

More bullets thudded through the window, smashing the remaining glass and ricocheting off the walls to spin round the inside of the room like wasps.

'Come on,' said Jost, retreating down the corridor. 'Let's get the rest.'

Suddenly his plan was going wrong. He'd lost Bernais and Grima, and for the first time he considered the possibility that he might fail in his mission.

'Upstairs,' he barked at Sinclair. 'Keep shooting. Keep them pinned down. Don't let them inside, or we'll be in trouble. I'm going for reinforcements.' The two men got to their feet and Sinclair rushed upstairs to get a better position, while Jost ran down to the cinema. He burst in, and ordered two of the remaining four men to get outside, while he ordered the remaining two to kill any of the hostages who moved.

As soon as the three of them were in the corridor, he explained what was happening.

'How many?' asked one of his remaining troops, another German who went by the pseudonym of the Count.

'God knows. Sinclair's on the upper level, keeping them pinned down. But we've got to stop them.

Bring out ten of the hostages. I warned those bastards on the mainland what would happen if they disobeyed my orders, and by Christ I'm going to show them I wasn't bluffing.'

The Count and the other terrorist, an ex-RAF pilot named Conway, whose job it was to fly the chopper off the rig, doubled back into the room, grabbed the ten hostages who were sitting closest to the door and bundled them back out at gunpoint. The rest of the prisoners started a low hum of conversation at what was happening, and Jost said: 'Shut up, or we'll shoot.' He looked at the two men whom he'd left to guard the prisoners, another American named Huston, and a Pole nicknamed Rocko. 'Do it if you have to,' he said.

Silence fell, and he left the room, slamming the door behind him, and headed upstairs.

Outside, the hostages were pushed back in the direction of the room that Jost and Sinclair had evacuated after Grima had been shot. From above, and from the open platform outside, the sound of gunfire could be heard, as Sinclair, from the vantage-point he'd found, was single-handedly preventing Valin's people from getting inside.

'Conway,' said Jost. 'Get up there and tell Sinclair to hold his fire. I want to talk to these people.'

Conway nodded, and made for the companion-way leading upwards.

'Walk out on to the platform,' Jost ordered the prisoners, as he and the Count hustled them into the room.

The hostages saw the debris of the short, one-sided fire-fight, and Grima's body lying spread-eagled on the floor where he had fallen, where snow, blown in by the wind through the broken window from outside, was already settling in the creases of his clothes, and stopped dead.

'Outside, I said,' barked Jost again. 'Or you'll all die here where you stand. Make your choice.'

The hostage at the front, a rigger named Newman, opened the door on to the platform, allowing more snow and wind into the room, stepped out into the light from the floods that Grima had switched on, his hands high in the air, as the fire from above and below died out. 'Don't shoot,' he screamed. 'We're unarmed.'

Jost ran to the broken window, and keeping in the cover of the wall beside it, yelled: 'Whoever you are outside, throw down your weapons and surrender, or we shoot these men.'

From where they had been taking cover from the shots that were coming from the control tower, Valin looked at his troops and said: 'Fuck.'

The prisoners stood together, shivering in the cold, covered from behind by Jost's men, and afraid to move a muscle in case the terrorists opened fire. Jost repeated his threat. 'I'm not bluffing,' he shouted. 'Whoever you are, throw down your weapons and surrender, or we shoot these men. I'll give you one minute.'

'What are we going to do, Colonel?' said Spenser, from where he lay next to Valin.

'Not surrender,' said Valin firmly.

'But what about those guys?'

'Too bad,' said the colonel. 'You and the rest are my main concern.'

'Colonel,' said Willis. 'I told you the civilians were the priority.'

'So we just cave in without a fight? Are you mad? We'll be the first to be killed. And who says he won't shoot the rest anyway?'

'I have my orders.'

'And I'm in charge here, remember?' Valin cut him off. 'If you want to surrender, do so. But my troops and I fight on.'

'You're time is almost up,' shouted Jost. 'This is your last chance.'

Suddenly one of the hostages made all discussion redundant. A fitter named Cantrell, a jockey-sized Geordie, broke ranks, and began to zigzag towards Valin and his party. The Count, who was holding an Uzi carbine cocked and ready to shoot, moved into the doorway and fired at the diminutive figure as he raced through the darkness. The bullets stitched a line up the back of his dirty overalls, blowing his stomach and lungs through the front of his body, and he skidded, face down, leaving a long, liquid, red smear in the snow, to stop just a few yards from the invading force. The rest of the hostages broke ranks too, and scattered in all directions as Jost and his companion sprayed them with a hail of bullets.

'Fire,' roared Valin, and his troops opened up with their weapons to try to give the hostages cover.

It wasn't clear to anyone exactly what was happening in the snowy darkness as the crew members tried to find some refuge from the flying lead that was coming at them from both directions, and both sets of soldiers were trying to kill each other.

But Valin's men had the numbers and fire-power, and gradually, mainly with the help of Spenser's Gatling's heavy bullets, they drove the terrorists who were defending the rig further back into the safety of the platform.

When the shooting from inside stopped, Valin held up his hand in the cease-fire gesture, and the platform fell silent.

'Angel. Recce,' ordered Valin. 'And be careful.'

'Why always me, Colonel?' asked the American. 'Don't you love me any more?'

'Just go.'

'Watch what's happening on top,' said Angel. 'I've only got one ass.'

'And a very pretty one it is too,' said Valin. 'So get it moving so we can all admire it.'

Angel snaked across the snow in the direction of the room that the shooting had come from. He could almost feel the bullets thudding into him as he went, and he was beginning to wish that he was anywhere but where he was.

He reached the open door, and peered inside, as the survivors of the ten hostages, reassured by the absence of shooting, slowly began to creep out from what cover they'd found.

The room inside was empty, and Angel got to his feet and beckoned his companions forward. As they cautiously got up, without coming under fire, Valin began to think that they might be in with a chance of winning.

'Who are you?' came a voice from beside him, as Newman, who'd led the prisoners out, and had managed to find a place of safety amid the gunfire, appeared at his side.

'The guys in white hats,' said Valin. 'Who are you?'

'Rigger Newman,' came the reply. 'They were going to kill us. Thanks.'

'Don't thank me,' said Valin, who refrained from telling Newman that he wouldn't have cared if the hostages *had* been shot. 'We were lucky. But your friend wasn't.' He indicated Cantrell's gutted body lying in a pool of blood that already had a crust of ice forming on its surface.

'A couple of the lads are bad,' said Newman. 'I think one or two of them copped it.'

'Get the rest inside,' ordered Valin. 'You'll freeze out here. Don't worry about the dead. They're past caring. And don't get in our way.' And he turned to go and check on his own troops.

Everyone was fine.

'Excellent,' said Valin. 'Let's get inside.'

Nevertheless the situation was dicey, but not desperate, as the return of fire towards Valin and his troops had stopped. He knew he had to be careful. And also they had the hostages in front of them as a human shield. It was hardly cricket as he'd been taught it at Harrow, but he had his people to think of. And as always, they came first.

'Fan out,' he ordered. 'Use all the cover you can get. O'Rourke, Spenser, Carmen, get inside after those civilians, and upstairs as best you can. The rest of us will be right behind you.'

'Sir,' said O'Rourke, and the three of them ducked and followed the dazed rig crew as they made their way towards the open door, where Angel was waiting, squatting down beside it, and keeping an eye out for anything happening inside.

But all was silent as the released prisoners cautiously went inside, closely followed by O'Rourke, Spenser and Carmen, O'Rourke roughly ordering the crew to get into one corner and stay out of everyone else's way. He ignored Grima's body, which stared up at the ceiling through sightless eyes, allowing only the single thought to cross his mind that there was now one less gunman to worry about.

He tried the door into the corridor outside, but

as he opened it, shells from a machine-pistol chewed at the metal and tore it out of his grasp, slamming it wide, and bouncing it back almost closed again.

'Shit,' he hissed, shaking his stinging hand. 'Bastards are waiting for us. Grenades. Everyone down, and protect your ears.' He pulled a fragmentation grenade from his jacket, flipped out the pin, and threw it through the gap between the door and the jamb.

Five seconds later it blew, springing wall sections from their frames, imploding glass, and doing damage to Sinclair, who, with Conway, had regrouped with Jost and the Count. The hot fragments of metal tore through his chest, neck and face, and knocked him to the floor, where he lay, emitting a high-pitched scream.

O'Rourke kicked the door all the way open and threw himself into the corridor, his silenced Scorpion burbling as he emptied a full magazine at the shadowy figures he could see where the corridor formed a 'T' with another.

The Count went down immediately, and Jost and Conway vanished behind the wall. O'Rourke threw himself into another doorway, almost tripping over Sinclair's body. By then he'd stopped screaming. Most of his face was gone, and his mouth was wide open and full of the blood that must have finally drowned him.

Spenser and Carmen came straight out of the door behind O'Rourke, and as soon as Spenser saw that he was in cover, he opened fire. His bullets ripped through the partitions at the end of the corridor, and he knew that anyone sheltering there would be cut to ribbons. After a short burst he stopped, both his and Carmen's ears ringing. O'Rourke popped his head out of the door at ground level, after reloading his carry gun. He waved, and ran along the corridor to the junction, knelt, then peered through the smoke from the explosions, first in the direction he'd seen the soldiers running, then the other way. There was no one in sight.

He beckoned for Spenser and Carmen to join him, and they set off to the left until they found a companion-way.

'Up or down?' asked Spenser.

'They stopped shooting from above, so I reckon there's no one there now. Let's go down,' said O'Rourke.

'You sure? The control tower, radio and radar are upstairs.'

'Sure I'm sure . . . Hell, I don't know. It's just a hunch.'

'OK,' said Spenser. 'Ready when you are.'

'Better wait for the others.'

'Here they come now,' said Carmen, as the rest of the men clattered around the corner after them.

'Let's do it then,' said O'Rourke. 'And good luck.'

18

O'Rourke had been half right. When Jost and Conway had themselves reached the companion-way, the German had sent the Englishman back to the cinema, with the order that the hostages should all be killed if it looked as if the invaders were winning, and that none of the terrorists should allow themselves to be taken alive.

Conway gave him an old-fashioned look on hearing the last instruction, but said nothing, just made his way down the stairs towards the cinema, while Jost headed up towards the radio room.

The German was filled with a mad fury, first that his men were losing the battle for the rig, and secondly, and even more importantly, that NP and the British government had both disobeyed his orders.

He slammed and locked the door of the radio shack behind him, pulling a heavy filing cabinet in front of it, and lowering the steel blinds that protected the windows. Down below he had three men and maybe forty hostages. He didn't care about them any longer. Or the ten million in ransom money. Money had never meant much to Jost, except as a tool to do more evil. But now it meant nothing. Something inside him had snapped when his plans had been thwarted and he'd lost his best and only friend to the invaders, because he knew for certain that Bernais was dead.

No, nothing mattered to him now, except that where he was up in the radio shack at the top of the control tower, he could be king of the castle. Especially with the knowledge that he held, of what he and the Frenchman had spent several hours that afternoon doing, unbeknown to any of the other men under his command.

When the terrorists had come on to the platform, Jost and Bernais had brought a quantity of plastic explosive with them – a large quantity. And they'd found the powder store on board the rig, which was well stocked with dynamite. Using that and the *plastique*, they'd planted enough explosive to blow the platform into the sea. The bombs had been armed with radio timers, which in turn were fired by the switches on the control box that Jost now held in his hand. Twelve switches, twelve timers, twelve explosions. Jost grinned at the thought, and counted as nothing the fact that he'd be blown to smithereens with the rig.

And if the invaders found the explosive packages? Jost's grin widened at the thought. The timers were specially designed by him, and if anyone touched them, they were rigged to blow up in their faces, and the charge of HE with them.

He reached for the microphone and called Aberdeen. 'Alpha Bravo Discovery to NP. Come in. Over.'

Conroy was waiting, as he had been all day. 'NP to Alpha Bravo Discovery. Receiving you strength ten. Over.'

'You had to do it, didn't you, Conroy? Over.'

'Do what? Over.'

'Don't fuck me around. You know very well. Send in a task force.'

'I have no knowledge, Alpha Bravo Discovery. Repeat: no knowledge of task force. Over.'

Jost thought for a moment before speaking again. 'You probably don't, little man. You're just a tiny cog in the capitalist machine. But today you're going to be a witness to what happens when the machine self-destructs.'

There was such a long pause that Conroy became alarmed. 'What's happening, Alpha Bravo Discovery? Come in, please. Over.'

'What's happening is that we were attacked by an armed force. And that means that you're about to find out what happens when one of these platforms drops into the sea. Over, and soon to be out for good.'

'No, Alpha Bravo Discovery. Please reconsider.' Conroy thought fast. 'What is the status of the crew? Over.'

'All dead, or soon will be. Plus the attack force. And my men. And me. Over.'

'Jost. Listen, please. The money is ready. You can have it whenever and wherever you want. Just don't blow the rig. Over.'

'Don't lie to me, Conroy. There's been enough of that already today. I offered you a straight deal. The rig and all on board in exchange for some cash. Probably about one per cent of your company's yearly profit. But someone had to be clever and do precisely what I told you not to do. So it's all over. All bets are off. The rig is primed to blow. I have the detonators with me. I can blow it manually or by timer. And if anyone messes with the charges, they go up there and then. You'd better let your people on board here know. If they don't want to die, they'd better get off the rig fast. Over and out.' And he punched the transmitter off.

'Alpha Bravo Discovery, come in, please,' repeated Conroy over and over again, but he knew there was no point. He was talking to air, and eventually reached for the direct line telephone to London, gritting his teeth as he did so.

Down in the cinema, Conway had found Rocko and Huston still guarding the remaining hostages.

'We're in deep shit,' he said, after he'd taken them out of earshot. 'There's a whole bunch of troops upstairs with heavy-duty automatic weapons. Christ knows where they came from. The whole deal's going sour. Jost wants us to fight to the last man, kill this lot, then ourselves, if it all fucks up. Which, believe me, it has. Well, the hell with that. I reckon it's every man for himself now. What do you guys say?'

'I say, where the hell's the chopper?' replied Huston.

'That's what I wanted to hear,' said Conway. 'The only trouble is, the weather's foul out there. I don't know if I can get it off the rig.'

'So what the fuck *do* we do?' asked Rocko.

'We give it our best shot,' replied Conway.

'What about this lot?' asked Huston, indicating the rig workers.

'What do we care?' was Conway's answer. 'We'll just lock them in here, and get the hell out of it ourselves.'

'Jost won't be happy,' said Rocko.

'The hell with him too,' said Conway. 'I signed on for this job for the money, not martyrdom.'

'And now the money's screwed?' said Rocko.

'It's all fucking screwed,' said Conway.

'I'm not sure I want to leave a load of people behind who might be able to identify me later,' said Rocko.

'That's the least of our worries right now,' said Conway. 'We've got to get off this heap of scrap iron first. Unless, of course, you want to kill all this lot by yourself. Me, I'm a pilot – not a mass murderer.'

Rocko looked at the forty or so men they were guarding. A hardened killer he might have been, but even he drew the line at shooting so many unarmed hostages. 'Fuck it,' he said. 'I guess you're right.'

'So let's go,' said Huston, and he made for the door.

But it was not going to be so easy. As he opened it, Spenser and Carmen hit the foot of the companion-way, and the American squeezed the trigger of the Gatling and stitched the wall and the door with a lethal line of lead.

Huston slammed the door shut again, and turned to his companions. 'What the hell do we do now?' he asked.

When Conroy got through to NP headquarters in London, and passed on Jost's message, the shit really hit the fan. Sir Jeremy Lion took the call personally. 'He's done *what*?' the MD exploded.

'He says he's rigged the platform to explode, sir,' repeated Conroy patiently. 'Either manually, or on timers. With the detonators fixed to blow if they're tampered with.'

'Did he say what time he's set them for?'

'No, sir.'

'And you didn't think to ask?' Sir Jeremy's tone was caustic.

'He cut me off before we'd got round to discussing that,' said Conroy. 'Would you care to hear the tape of the conversation for yourself?'

'No,' said the MD curtly. 'I wouldn't.'

'I don't think he was joking,' said Conroy. 'Are you going to inform Whitehall?'

'I'll do whatever I think fit,' said Sir Jeremy.

'We could lose the rig.'

'It's well insured.'

Conroy couldn't believe what he was hearing. 'But all the men . . .'

'That's my responsibility, not yours,' said Sir Jeremy, and slammed down the phone.

He reached for the direct line to Bryant-Marshall, then hesitated, weighing up the pros and cons of what he'd just heard.

OK, so the rig was going to be destroyed. But was that entirely a bad thing? It was fully covered by Lloyd's, who may have been going through a bad time recently but certainly had enough money to cover the loss. So what if a few more 'names' went bankrupt, or committed suicide as a result? They should have thought about the risk before they became involved. Just because the bloody fools thought it was the licence to print money it had once been. The company might even make a profit on the deal with a bit of luck. Alpha Bravo Discovery hadn't been performing very well recently, and there'd even been talk of closing it down in the near future.

And as for the crew, Sir Jeremy reflected, well, there were plenty more roughnecks willing to risk their lives in ridiculous conditions for shockingly low wages. The unemployment rate for oil workers in Scotland was a national disgrace. Sir Jeremy had remarked on the fact at dinner with the Prime Minister only the previous week. And any compensation awards to them were covered by Lloyd's too. But on the upside, there was the ten million in used notes that the accountants were busily beavering away collecting. That wasn't covered by anyone. Nor was the million he'd promised the mercenaries. All that could be saved by one finger on one detonator button. And Jost and his bombs would certainly make sure that no one lived to tell the tale.

Yes, thought the MD, as he pulled his hand back from the telephone. All in all it might not be a bad thing if the rig was blown to pieces. And as for Conroy, promotion and a decent bonus would keep him quiet. And if it didn't there were certain people that Sir Jeremy was aware of who would do the job for a very small sum of money. The only problem was the tape of the conversation between Conroy and Jost. It would be much better if that were in his possession as soon as possible. So, instead of phoning Bryant-Marshall, he called Conroy again in Aberdeen.

This time his voice was silky as he said: 'My apologies for being so brusque earlier. I'm afraid this whole business has got to me more than I'd thought.'

'Think nothing of it, sir,' said Conroy, rather surprised at his MD's change of manner.

205

'Decisions are being made about the best way of treating Jost's threats,' said Sir Jeremy. 'But we mustn't be panicked into any premature course of action. And we do need the tapes of all your conversations with the rig. Can you get them on to the next domestic flight down. Send one of your people as a courier. Someone you can trust.'

'Of course, sir,' said Conroy.

'Good. I'll be in touch with you again soon. Keep monitoring the radio. And thanks for your sterling work today.'

'It's my job, sir.'

'Believe me, it won't go unrewarded. You've got my word on that.'

'Thank you, sir.'

'No. Thank *you*.' Sir Jeremy replaced the phone on the hook and leant back in his chair, perfectly satisfied with the way things were going.

The hostages in the cinema were grouped together at one end. This was the first they knew that the rig was in the process of being liberated, and they talked together, quietly but excitedly, at the prospect of freedom. Conway approached the nearest hostage, a fitter named Johnny Bates. 'Is there another way out of here?' he asked.

'Work it out for yourself,' said Bates.

Conway cocked the gun he was holding and stuck it into Bates's face. 'Don't fuck me about, son,' he said. 'You don't know how close you

206

lot are to an early grave. Now is there another
way out?'

Bates stared blankly at him for a moment, then
said: 'Behind the screen. There's an air-conditioning
outlet. It leads on to the platform. It's narrow, but
will take a man. All you have to do is pull off the
screen this end, crawl down, then kick the screen
out at the other.'

'Is it close to the helipad?'

'Right underneath it.'

'Fine,' said Conway. Then he returned to Huston
and Rocko. 'We can get outside through a duct at
the back,' he said.

'Let's do it, then,' said Rocko.

The hostages looked at them as they went behind
the cinema screen, but said nothing. Then, as soon
as the trio of terrorists had vanished, Bates said to
one of the other men: 'Give me your shirt, Nick. I
need a white flag. Don't want my head shot off.'

The man tugged his shirt off, and Bates went
to the door with it. He pulled the door open and
threw out the shirt, as a blast of fire rang out from
down the corridor, and bullets slammed into the
door-frame.

At the sight of the white material, Valin, who was
watching from the safety of a doorway, signalled
for a cease-fire. 'If this is a trick, you'll pay for
it,' he yelled, and gestured for one of the MPs to
move down. 'If anyone as much as looks sideways
at you, blast 'em,' he shouted, then he had Angel

leap-frog him drop into cover to allow Willis to make the doorway of the cinema. Slowly he pushed it open and Bates, his hands high in the air, said: 'They've gone.'

'Where?' said Willis, pushing the door all the way open.

'Behind the screen. Through an air-conditioning duct. They're going for the helicopter, I think.'

'How many?' asked Valin as he came through the door, closely followed by the rest.

'Three.'

'Is Jost with them?'

'Who?'

'The leader.'

'No. We haven't seen him since he took out ten of our mates earlier on. Are they all right?'

'Most of them,' said Valin. Then to the MPs: 'You two. Get after them. We'll try and cut them off at the pass.'

The two men did as they were told, and the rest turned and ran back the way they'd come, and made for the closest exit to the outside of the platform.

The three terrorists, meanwhile, had reached the outside, and Conway, who by this time had assumed command, ordered them to replace the screen on the duct and watch it for any sign of pursuit. Meanwhile he climbed up the outside of the platform to where the twelve-seater Sikorsky was waiting, rendered a hump of white by its layer of snow, and only recognizable for what it was by its rotors, bent almost to the surface of the helipad by their own layers of ice.

Bryers and Smith, the two MPs, had found the first cover lying on the floor beside the opening to the air-conditioning duct, and slid inside, carry weapons to the fore, then inched their way along the cold metal of the floor towards the outside world.

The remaining eight invaders raced along the narrow corridors of the inside of the platform until they found an exit door. O'Rourke slammed it open, and with his Scorpion cocked and ready, poked his head out into the teeth of the wind. When nothing happened, he moved on to the metal floor of the platform, and spun on his heels in the thick layer of snow that lay upon it, looking up for the helipad. Through the gloom he saw a dark figure knocking snow from the windscreen of the Sikorsky. He hesitated, his finger on the trigger, afraid that at the distance and angle, with the visibility as it was, and with the short-range weapon he was using, he'd have little chance of a clean shot. He hesitated just long enough for Rocko, who by then had spotted him, to fire off a burst in his direction, which went wide for the same reasons that had made O'Rourke hold his fire, but nevertheless forced the lieutenant back the way he'd come.

'There's someone up by the chopper,' O'Rourke said to Valin. 'And at least another one's got his bead on the exit.'

'So I noticed,' said Valin drily. 'You almost lost your head there, Mark. Spenser, Carmen, McCall, find another exit, and try and get them in some crossfire. There can only be two at the most watching the doors, if the third's checking on the 'copter. But watch out for Jost. He's got to be about somewhere. Go. And watch your backs.'

The three of them turned as one and headed down the corridor in the direction they'd all been going. At that moment Bryers, who was in front of Smith, after losing a toss of the coin to decide who'd go first, came to the screen at the far end of the air-conditioning duct. It was bent out of shape, and dotted with ice from where the terrorists had knocked it out of its clips, and Bryers wasn't happy about it being replaced. If the terrorists had fled, he figured quite rightly, they would just have left it where it lay. 'Reckon there's a welcoming committee?' he whispered over his shoulder to Smith.

'Count on it.'

'Right, I'm out of here. Don't follow until the coast's clear.'

'Don't worry about that. I'm as snug as a bug here. I always did do well with heads or tails.'

'Too fucking right. I reckon that coin you use is well bent.' He hesitated for a moment, then said: 'Sod it. Here I go.'

'Good luck, son,' said Smith.

'Believe me, I need it,' said Bryers, and powered himself forward, smashing the screen out of its clips again, and dived headlong into the drift of snow that had collected around the opening.

Huston fired at him point-blank as he tried desperately to find cover. The bullets ripped through his body, staining the snow red, as Rocko fired his automatic weapon into the duct, blowing Smith's head almost off his shoulders.

'Anyone else in there, you reckon?' said Rocko, when they'd exhausted their magazines and ducked back into cover to reload.

'They're mincemeat if they are,' replied Huston. 'And the guy you killed won't be easy to get past.'

'Good shooting,' said Rocko, looking at Bryers's still form. 'That's two of the bastards who won't be going home.'

And nor would he, as Spenser, Carmen and McCall, who by then had found an alternative exit and had been alerted to Rocko and Huston's position by the sound of their gunfire, started shooting themselves, their first volley smashing into the Pole's body and knocking him to the ground.

Huston turned his weapon on the three of them, and his first spray of bullets knocked McCall off his feet, before O'Rourke, McGough, Angel, Valin and Willis, who had been waiting inside their exit, pushed the door open and sprayed lead in the direction from which Rocko had fired at O'Rourke. Huston, caught in the crossfire, had no chance, and the heavy-calibre rounds from Spenser's and

Carmen's Gatling caught the American, and sent him flying backwards in a macabre dance of death, before he too joined his companion on the floor of the platform.

Carmen knelt by McCall's still form, and felt for a pulse. It was weak, but he was still alive, and she and her husband dragged him back inside.

Valin and his four companions surfed across the snow in their direction, McGough stopping to check for vital signs from the four bodies that had gone down in the short but fierce battle around the air-conditioning duct. But there were none. Bryers and Smith, and the two terrorists whose names were unknown to Angel, were all dead, the snow already lying on the three in the open air, and blowing in on Smith, who lay inside the conduit.

The colonel, Willis and O'Rourke joined Spenser and Carmen beside McCall's body. Willis knelt down and touched his friend's face. It was waxy and cold, and he looked up at the colonel and said: 'There must be something we can do for him.'

Valin, who had seen too many men die before, shook his head. McCall's face was turning blue, and a dark-red stain was spreading across his jacket as his life's blood drained away.

'I'm sorry,' he said. 'I don't think there's anything. He needs a hospital and an intensive-care unit. It's out of our hands now.'

'Fuck that bastard Jost,' said Willis, coming to his feet. 'Where the hell is he?'

McCall made a rattling sound in his chest, and his breathing became stertorous as he drew closer to death.

'We should put him out of his misery,' said Angel to Willis. 'Man, it's cruel to leave him like this.'

'I'm not going to leave him,' said Willis.

'We're not staying here,' said Valin. 'If you won't do it, I will.' And he reached for his side-arm.

'No,' said Willis, and made as if to turn his gun on the colonel, before O'Rourke pushed the barrel of his Scorpion into Willis's chest.

'You're too ready to point your gun at us,' he said. 'It could seriously shorten your life expectancy. We're supposed to be on the same side, remember?'

But then, as if to preclude any further argument, McCall opened his eyes and said quite clearly: 'Let them kill me, Toby. It hurts too much.' Then he coughed a great gout of blood over his front, turned his head to one side and died.

'End of story,' said Angel. 'Now let's go and finish this fucking job. I want to go home.'

19

At NP headquarters in Aberdeen, Conroy was thinking more and more about the strange and uncharacteristic call from Sir Jeremy Lion in London. It didn't make sense, he thought. Not after the previous one, where the MD had been so unpleasant. And he hadn't trusted the oily tones that Lion had assumed in the latter conversation. And why the hell did he need the tapes of Conroy's conversations with Jost on the rig? It all seemed very suspicious to the man sitting in the radio room in Scotland.

The more Conroy pondered, the more it struck him that something was seriously wrong. And that whatever it was threatened the workers on Alpha Bravo Discovery, many of whom were his personal friends, as well as the brave men who had made the second assault on the rig, in an attempt to recapture it.

He tried calling Jost again, but to no avail. The German wasn't answering.

Shit. What the hell do I do now? he thought. And then he picked up the direct line that had been set up to Bryant-Marshall's office, and kissed his career goodbye.

'Yes,' said Bryant-Marshall, when he picked up his phone.

'Conroy here, sir. Has Sir Jeremy been in touch?'

'Since when?'

'During the last half hour or so.'

'No.'

'Jesus,' said Conroy. 'I think there's something you should know.'

When he'd finished telling Bryant-Marshall about his talk with Jost, the man from Whitehall said: 'Do you still have the tapes?'

'Yes.'

'Good. Don't let them out of your sight.'

'Sir Jeremy is expecting them down in London this evening.'

'He'll be lucky,' said Bryant-Marshall. 'Nothing's left Aberdeen airport since this morning. Tell him you've sent a courier down by road. That'll keep him quiet until the morning. And by then I expect the die will be cast one way or the other.'

'Very well,' said Conroy.

'I don't expect you'll have much of a future with NP after this.'

'Or any other oil company,' said Conroy. 'But I couldn't live with myself if any of my friends died because of my job prospects.'

'Don't worry. You've done the right thing. I might have something for you myself. A little integrity wouldn't go amiss down here. How do you fancy relocating to the soft south of England?'

'I wouldn't mind that at all, sir.'

'Then just carry on like you're doing, and I'll see what I can do.' His voice got more serious as he said: 'And you have no idea what time Jost has set the charges for.'

'No, sir.'

'Right. Well, keep trying the platform, and I'll get through to the sub so that the captain can send a message to the men on the rig.'

'Thank God for that.'

'No problem, Conroy. We'll talk later. Good-bye.'

What webs we all weave, Bryant-Marshall thought to himself as he looked at his watch. And what lies we all tell. And decided it was time for dinner. He put on his overcoat and as he passed through the outer office, where his faithful secretary was still on duty, he said: 'If anyone needs me I'll be at my club.'

'There's still at least one outside,' said O'Rourke, after Willis had covered McCall's face with his own jacket. 'By the chopper.'

'Do you think it's Jost, trying to get away?' said Spenser.

'Christ knows.'

'He'll have a hell of a job in this weather. It'll be bloody suicidal.'

'Maybe he's trying to disable the thing.'

'Then maybe we'd better go and have a shufti,' said Valin. 'Any transport at all might come in handy later.'

Now down to seven hands, the mercenaries made their way out into the open again, where the force of the weather hadn't lessened, but, if anything, was fiercer than before.

'Chrissakes,' said Angel, as the full force of the bitter Arctic wind hit him full on. 'Why the hell did I ever leave California? I never was one for winter sports.'

'God knows,' replied Spenser, who was next to him. 'You'll know better next time.'

'You can say that again,' said his fellow American.

'Shut up,' said Valin. 'And spread out. Approach the chopper from the rear. I'd like to take at least one of these monkeys alive. Especially if it *is* Jost.'

'Understood, Colonel,' said Spenser, as the group fanned out through the blizzard, and made their way up to the helipad.

As they peered through the blizzard, they could all see that at least some attempt had been made to clear the weight of snow off the big Sikorsky. They padded silently up behind it, and Angel tried the side door with his hand. It was stiff with ice, but after he applied some pressure he felt it give, and raised his thumb. Gingerly he slid it slowly open and climbed inside the helicopter, glad of what little respite the thin hull gave against the wind. The passenger section was empty, and the door to the flight deck was shut. He made his way quietly up the narrow aisle between the seats, until he reached it, then gently he tried that door too. It slid silently open, and he saw a figure sitting in the pilot's seat hunched over the controls. He touched the barrel of his carry weapon against the back of the figure's neck and whispered: 'Relax, doc, or I'll blow your fuckin' head off.'

The figure stiffened and tried to turn round, but Angel increased the pressure and said: 'Let's see your hands, sweetheart. I'd hate to redecorate the inside of this crate with your brains.'

Conway slowly raised his empty hands above his head.

'Good,' said Angel, and called back through the open door: 'Come on in, fellas. The water's fine.'

The rest of the group squeezed into the hull of the chopper, and Valin went into the flight deck.

'Name,' he demanded.

The British pilot looked at him and said: 'Guess.'

Angel hit him on the back of his head with the barrel of his Uzi and growled: 'You might as well tell us, pal. You will in the end. You'll be the only one to suffer on the way. Save yourself some grief and come clean.'

Conway looked at the hard faces of the two men crowded into the cockpit with him, and the others peering through from the passenger section, and decided that discretion was the better part of valour. 'Conway,' he said.

'And your job?' Valin again.

'I'm a flyer. Ex-RAF. My job was to get our men off in this thing.'

'Looks like you've got very few men left,' remarked Valin. 'We've just dealt with two more of them.'

Conway shrugged. 'That's pretty much it, then.'

'How many of you were there? And tell me the truth. Because if at any point I find you've been lying, we'll deal with you too. Be honest, and you might come out of this with your skin intact.'

'Nine,' said Conway.

Valin did some quick mental arithmetic. 'That means there's just two of you left alive: you and Jost.'

'And he's the most dangerous one of the lot,' said Conway. 'He wanted the rest of us to kill ourselves rather than allow ourselves to be captured.'

'But you didn't go along with that idea,' said Angel laconically.

'I value my skin,' replied Conway.

'Very wise,' said Valin. 'So where is Jost?'

'God knows. He might be anywhere on this damn piece of glorified scaffolding. But watch him. *He* won't give in without a fight. I always knew I was mad to get involved in his stupid scheme.'

'But it seemed like a good idea at the time,' said Valin.

'Easy money. At least until you lot came along. Where the hell did you spring from anyway? How did you get organized so quickly?'

'From the bowels of a big silver fish,' said Angel. 'We were at another party and we just couldn't resist coming to yours too.' Then to Valin: 'So what now, Colonel?'

'Back inside the rig and try and find Jost. We'd better round up the crew and get a message through to the submarine. Our job's almost over here, and we should get some sort of evacuation under way.' He looked around the inside of the chopper. 'Will this thing fly, Conway?'

'It'll fly OK,' the pilot said. 'But not under these circumstances. Look for yourself' – he pointed through the windscreen, which he'd partially cleared on the outside, but which was already covered with a rime of fresh snow – 'it's a no-no until the weather clears.'

'Back inside the rig, then,' said Valin. 'And everyone. Remain alert. None of us should relax until Jost is ours or dead.'

They all exited the helicopter after Angel had searched Conway for weapons and confiscated the handgun he was carrying, then moved back across the helipad and through the inside of the rig towards the cinema where were congregated the men they'd left behind, plus the survivors of the ten that Jost had pulled out earlier.

'Who's in charge here?' asked Valin, when they

walked in the room. The crewmen fell silent and looked at each other. Then Tom Fowler, the rig boss, stepped forward. 'I am,' he said. 'Who exactly are you?'

'Rag, Tag and Bobtail,' said Valin. 'We were sent here by Her Majesty's Government, and your superiors in London, to recapture the rig. This we seem to have done in essence. Except for one slight problem: we seem to be missing the leader of the gang who hijacked your rig. Jost is his name, and he's a very dangerous man – made all the more dangerous by the fact that his plans have been thwarted. We need to get a message though to the submarine that brought us here, and our radio is kaput. Where's the radio room?'

'On top,' said Fowler. 'That was where he and his mate were holed up earlier.'

'Which mate?' asked Angel.

'A big French bloke.'

'Don't worry about him,' said Spenser. 'He's out of the picture.'

'I told you he's on his own,' said Valin. 'We'd better go and check the radio shack. Fowler, show us the way. The rest of you stay here with our prisoner.' He saw the looks on the men's faces. 'And don't let any harm befall him. He may come in handy later.'

There were rumbles of discontent from the men, but Valin ignored them, and he, Fowler and the rest left the cinema.

'Stay at the back,' the colonel said to the rig boss. 'We're dealing with a potential madman here.'

As silently as possible, the eight of them made their way up towards the radio room in the control tower. When they got close, Fowler saw that the shutters were down and said: 'He's probably in there. He's lowered the steel protectors.'

'Damn,' said Valin. 'Is there another way in?'

'Only from out on the platform. And he can lock all the doors. It'd be almost impossible to storm the place.'

'We could grenade the doors,' said Angel. 'And chew the shit out of the place with the Gatling.'

Spenser nodded.

'Not so fast,' said Valin. 'We don't know what surprises he's got up his sleeve.' Then to Fowler: 'Is there a phone in there?'

'Of course.'

'Where's there another one?'

'There are phones on every landing,' explained Fowler. 'I'll show you.' They made their way back down the short flight of steps they'd just climbed, to where a boxed handset was mounted on the wall.

'Number?' demanded Valin.

'Two-o-one,' replied Fowler, and Valin dialled the number.

When the telephone in the radio shack rang, Jost jumped slightly, and crushed out his cigarette on the side of the table. He looked at the handset and smiled to himself. So it is almost over, he thought, as he picked it up.

'Yes,' he said.

'Jost?' said Valin.

'At your service. But you have me at a disadvantage. You obviously know my name. But to whom am *I* speaking?'

'Colonel James Valin, late of the British SAS. Now in command of the strike force that has recaptured oil rig Alpha Bravo Discovery.'

'Not quite recaptured, Colonel,' said Jost. 'You have me to deal with first.'

'And you have *us* to deal with,' said Valin crisply. 'I must assume that you are on your own . . .' He let the words hang in the air.

'Assume what you will, Colonel,' said Jost. 'But please don't assume that I am powerless.'

'We could blow you and the radio room to hell without very much trouble,' said Valin. 'So why don't you just open up, throw out any weapons you have in there, and come out with your hands in the air.'

'I think you've been watching too many American films, Colonel,' said Jost. 'Has no one been in contact with you from the mainland?'

'No,' said Valin.

'How very odd,' said the German with a smile to himself, then asked: 'Have you by any chance taken a close look around the rig?'

'What do you mean?'

'What I say. I can only assume that you haven't. Because if you had, you might have noticed that I have made some modifications to it.'

'What kind of modifications?' Valin said, his hackles rising at Jost's words.

'Only the most basic type. I have planted a dozen charges of high explosive. Look carefully and you'll probably find them. But only look, Colonel. Don't touch, whatever you do. The detonators are of a special design of mine. You fool around with any of them, and they'll set off the charges. They're all on timers, and I can detonate them from in here too. One touch from me, and the rig goes. So I don't think your idea of blowing me to hell is a very good one. The minute you try, the rig goes, and you, me, your people and the rig crew with it.'

'I see,' said Valin, with more aplomb than he felt. 'And what time have you set them for?'

'For now that will remain my little secret. So why don't you have a think about things, Colonel, and call me back. I'm not going anywhere in the foreseeable future.' And with that Jost put down the phone at his end and lit another cigarette.

'Damn,' said Valin as he put the receiver back on its hook.

'What's up, boss?' asked Angel.

'The lunatic's set a dozen charges of explosive all over the rig,' replied Valin grimly. 'The detonators are booby-trapped, they're on timers, and he can blow them from inside the room where he's holed up. The bastard's suicidal.'

'Christ,' said Fowler. 'You can't let him get away with that.'

'Seems like he already has,' said Valin drily. 'What do you suggest?'

Fowler didn't answer.

'What time?' asked Angel, as usual getting right to the heart of the problem. 'When are we due to be blown to kingdom come?'

'He wouldn't say,' replied Valin.

'Course he won't,' interjected McGough. 'Did you really think he would?'

Valin shook his head.

'Do you know where he's laid the charges?' asked Fowler.

'Just around,' said Valin. 'That's all he'd tell me. I think he expects us to play hide-and-seek.'

'Then let's do it. Let's try and find one,' said the rig boss. 'I've had some experience with explosives. In the job, you know,' he added. 'I might be able to do something.'

'Like send us all to an early grave,' said Angel.

'Any other ideas?' said Willis.

'Get off this heap fast, and leave our buddy Jost, or whatever his name is, to blow himself and it into the sea,' replied the young American. 'What the hell do we care? It's not our problem.'

'We agreed to try and do a job,' said Valin. 'I think we should make more of a go of it.'

Angel thought for a moment, then grinned. 'Yeah, Colonel. You're right as usual. What the hell? I'd only waste the rest of my life trying to get rid of the dough we're getting, as fast as I can. Let's make like John Wayne and see what we can see.'

Valin turned to Fowler. 'If you were going to try and place explosives to do the most damage, where would you start?'

The rig boss thought for a second or two. 'The boiler room,' he said. 'On the lowest level. The heart of the rig. You could do a lot of damage there with a quite small charge.'

'Show us then,' said Valin. 'And let's get some of your oppos to have a look round too.'

'Do you think that dude Conway knows where the charges are?' asked Spenser.

'There's only one way to find out,' replied Valin.

The eight returned to the cinema, where Conway was sitting in one corner smoking a cigarette. Valin went straight over to him, leaving Fowler to explain what was happening to his men.

'Thank Christ you're here,' said Conway, who was sweating slightly, although the room was chilly. 'They were talking lynch parties a minute ago.'

'Can you blame them?' said Valin. 'What do you know about these explosive charges?'

'What?' said Conway, with such surprise in his voice that Valin instinctively knew he wasn't lying. 'What are you talking about?'

The colonel explained, and Conway started to sweat even harder. 'Jesus,' he said. 'I knew Jost was crazy. But not this crazy.'

Valin looked over to where Fowler was talking to his men. 'There might be more talk of a lynch party now.'

'You'll protect me, won't you?' There was genuine fear in Conway's voice.

Valin looked at the flyer with disgust. 'Oh yes. Don't worry about that. We'll protect you.'

Fowler came over and joined the pair of them. 'I've told my blokes,' he said. 'They're not too happy with this one.' He gestured at Conway. 'Specially after what happened to a couple of their mates. But they'll leave him alone for now. We're going to split into small teams and look round the rig.'

'Fine,' said Valin. 'But tell them to look – not to touch. And make sure a couple of them stay here and look after our friend. We don't want him wandering off, do we? Meanwhile, you take me and my troops down to the boiler room.'

Fowler nodded, designated a couple of sturdy riggers to take care of Conway, then led Valin and his six companions down into the bowels of the platform and the boiler room. It was pitch-dark inside, and he found some switches and turned on the heavy-duty fluorescent striplights. 'Anywhere in here,' he said, and started to check the shadowy corners of the place. Valin's people started hunting too, but it was Fowler, a minute or so later, who shouted: 'Over here.'

Everyone crowded round as he pointed to where a dark bundle, wrapped in a black garbage sack, was sitting wedged between one of the boilers and the temperature gauge next to it. 'That shouldn't be there,' he said.

He gently touched the bundle to reveal a black plastic box on top of it, connected to half a dozen sticks of dynamite by three differently coloured wires.

'That's enough,' said Valin. 'So now we know he was telling the truth.'

'What shall we do?' asked Fowler.

'Leave the bloody thing alone, and go and talk to Jost again.'

When they got back to the cinema, about half of Fowler's teams had returned, all of them reporting finding suspicious bundles identical to the one that Fowler had discovered, hidden at vital points all over the oil platform. Nine in all.

'So we're missing three,' said Valin. 'Not that that matters. They'll probably turn up. We're not even going to think about trying to disarm them. I need a phone again.'

'In my office upstairs,' said the rig boss. 'You'll be more comfortable there. And there's a bottle of good malt in one of the desk drawers. Fancy a dram?'

'I thought you'd never ask,' said Valin, and the

two men went off, leaving everyone else to wait impatiently.

On the way Valin said: 'I have to get through to that bloody submarine. Are there any other radios on board?'

'Sure,' said Fowler. 'There's one in the chopper. Or you could call my office in Aberdeen, and they could pass the message on. We do have satellite phones here.'

'Christ,' said Valin, 'I must be getting old. I forgot about the new technology.'

'Not all *that* new,' said Fowler.

'Right. That's great. I can call anyone?'

'Anyone in the world.'

'Very good,' said Valin, as Fowler showed him into a comfortably appointed office, and took a bottle from the desk as promised. When both men had a glass, Valin sat behind Fowler's desk, picked up the phone and punched three keys.

Jost answered on the second ring.

'Valin,' said the colonel.

'How *are* things, Colonel?' said Jost.

'Precisely as you described.'

'Good. I can tell by the fact that we're all still alive that you haven't interfered with them.'

'Yes.'

'Good.'

'So what now?'

'Now, Colonel, the boot, as you English say, is on the other foot. Now it's your turn to surrender to me. I'm looking forward to meeting you in the flesh.'

'You are joking.'

'Not at all. And don't think about trying any tricks. Unless you are standing alone, in front of the door here in two minutes, I blow the rig out of the water.'

'Wait a minute,' said Valin, rising from his seat.

'No. *You* wait a minute, and we're all dead,' said Jost. 'Time is ticking away, even as we speak.'

Now standing, Valin threw the phone back on its hook. 'He wants me upstairs,' he said to Fowler, unbuckling the holster around his waist and tossing his knife on to the desk next to it. 'I have about ninety seconds to get there or he's threatening to blow the charges.'

'And you're going?' asked Fowler incredulously. 'He may kill you.'

'I have no choice. If I don't, he may kill us all. Get downstairs and inform my second in command, Lieutenant O'Rourke. Tell him he has to assume command now. Tell him to do what has to be done. And tell him about the radio in the chopper and the telephones.'

'No go on the phones, I'm afraid,' said Fowler. 'Jost must've messed with the equipment. All the lines are dead. I was trying the outside connections while you were on the phone to him.'

'I had a feeling he might have,' said Valin. 'But I'd better be out of here. Fast.'

'Do you want me to come with you?'

'No. I'll handle this on my own. Get O'Rourke to call the radio shack. I want him to know as much about what Jost has planned for us as possible. Now go. Otherwise we might all meet a watery fate – sooner rather than later.'

Valin ran from the room in the direction of the control tower. He met no one on the way, and slid to a halt outside the door barely a minute after he'd left Fowler's office. He rapped hard on the panels, and a voice from behind him, deep in the shadows at a junction of corridors, said: 'Go right in, the door's not locked. I'm glad to see you came alone, and so promptly.' Jost moved into the light, a huge Uzi Desert Eagle automatic pistol in one fist, the detonator box in the other hand, and an unlit cigarette between his teeth. 'I take it you know what this is,' Jost said, his eyes flicking to the box and back to Valin.

'I know.'

'Then step lightly, Colonel. One touch and we're history.'

'I understand.'

'Get inside.'

Valin entered the radio room, which was large and spartan. The radio was showing several red lights, but was silent.

'I take it you're unarmed,' said Jost, then followed Valin inside, shut the door behind him, put the detonator box carefully on a table and slipped the locks on the door.

'I am,' said Valin.

'But better to be safe than sorry. Come here,' said Jost. When Valin complied, he expertly patted the colonel down for any concealed weapons, the Uzi all the time steadily pointed at Valin's head, and Jost's eyes not once leaving his. 'Very good, Colonel,' he said when he was satisfied. 'They taught you to obey orders well. Where was it? Sandhurst?'

Valin nodded.

'Please sit down,' said Jost, indicating a swivel chair on castors in one corner of the room.

Valin sat and almost immediately the phone on the desk by the radio table rang. It rang twice more, but Jost ignored it.

'Aren't you going to answer it?' asked Valin calmly.

'It's probably for you.'

'May I, then?'

Jost shook his head and answered it himself, the gun held unwaveringly in his hand.

'Hold on,' he said after a moment, then to Valin: 'I was right. Someone called O'Rourke.' He put the phone back on the hook.

Down in the cinema, O'Rourke looked at his friends and said: 'Bastard's hung up. But I heard him speak to the colonel, so *he's* all right. At least for now.'

'Thank God for that,' said Carmen.

'What do we do now?' asked McGough.

'Get these civilians off the rig. Spenser, will you go and try and raise the sub on the radio in the chopper. I hope it's still working, but Jost may have removed some vital part. He seems pretty thorough. Take Carmen with you.'

Spenser nodded, and he and Carmen left the room, leaving the Gatling and carrying their side-arms cocked and ready to fire.

Then O'Rourke beckoned Fowler over. 'Are there procedures to completely evacuate the rig in case of a serious accident or some such eventuality?' he asked.

'Sure,' replied the rig boss. 'We've got pontoons slung under the platform with enough space for everyone. You climb on board, buckle yourself in, hit a switch, and they drop into the sea. It's quite an experience. You drop nearly a hundred feet. Can be quite a shock when you hit the water. It's like landing on cement.'

'And they're OK?'

'As far as I know. I can't see any reason for Jost and his gang to mess with them.'

'Do you want to check them out.'

'We're staying.'

'No, Mr Fowler,' said O'Rourke. 'I'm sorry, but you can't. We're being paid to do this job. And you'd just be in the way. Excess to our requirements, as it were. Besides, part of our brief was to get as many of you off unharmed as we could.'

Fowler hesitated, then nodded and said: 'I'll go and look at them.'

He was gone for perhaps ten minutes, during which time all was quiet from the control tower.

He came back into the cinema and said to O'Rourke: 'They look good.'

'Good. I'm going to try the radio room again.' And O'Rourke picked up the phone and called the number once more.

Jost picked the telephone up after the fourth ring and listened without speaking.

'O'Rourke again, Mr Jost. Please don't hang up.'

'Speak to me,' said Jost.

'I wish to evacuate the civilian crew from the rig. I don't want to alarm you in any way or make out we're playing any tricks. Do I have your permission?'

'Certainly. I care nothing for those poor capitalist lackeys. In fact I think I would prefer to be left here with Colonel Valin alone. We can watch the sunrise. Metaphorically, of course. And then go and meet our maker together. I recognize the colonel as a kindred soul. If I have to die, and it appears that I do, I want to be with a fellow-soldier – someone who will face eternity with me with equanimity. So I would prefer it if everyone left – you and your people included. There is really no point in you

234

staying. It would be futile for you to attempt to try to release him. All of you would die with us. Do you understand?'

Barking mad, thought O'Rourke as he squeezed the receiver tightly in his hand. 'Yes, sir,' he said. 'But could I have a brief word with the colonel before we go?'

'I suppose so,' said Jost. Then to Valin: 'He wants to make his farewells.'

Valin stood up, walked over to Jost and took the phone from his hand.

'We're not leaving you here,' said O'Rourke.

'Yes you are,' said Valin.

'But Colonel.'

'He's right. You wouldn't have a ghost of a chance of getting in here. Get everyone off the rig. At least then, you'll be safe.'

'But . . .'

'No buts, Mark. Take that as a direct order.'

Jost snatched the receiver from Valin's hand. 'You heard what he said, didn't you?' he barked into the phone.

'Yes,' said O'Rourke, quietly.

'Then do it. And don't call again.' With that Jost put the phone down. 'Alone at last,' he said to Valin.

'Son of a bitch,' said O'Rourke as he dropped the phone back on its stand.

'What?' said McGough.

'He's ordered everyone off the rig – us included.

235

But the colonel stays. And then he takes him with him when he blows the rig.'

'Like hell.'

'And the colonel's confirmed it. It's an order.'

'Under duress. You're not seriously thinking of leaving.'

'What do you think?'

Before O'Rourke could answer, Spenser and Carmen came back into the cinema. 'The radio's fine on the chopper,' said Spenser. 'But we can't raise a thing from the sub.'

'Probably fucked off and left us,' said Angel, who didn't notice the look in Willis's eye that said he might just be right.

'Why not let me go and have a try?' said Willis. 'I raised them before, on the island.'

'Why not?' said O'Rourke. 'Just watch yourself.'

Willis left the room. After he'd gone, O'Rourke filled Spenser and Carmen in on what Jost had said on the phone.

'Fuck that,' said Spenser. 'I'm not leaving him here.'

'Don't worry, we won't,' said O'Rourke. 'We get these civilians off the rig – and you as well, McGough – but the rest of us stay. If we keep our heads down, Jost will think we've gone too, and relax. Then we can grab him and get the colonel back.'

'Why me?' interjected McGough.

'Because your mission here is over. It's up to us now.'

'As long as Jost doesn't realize we're still on the platform and blow it to kingdom come,' said Angel.

'Then it's our job to make sure that he doesn't,' said Spenser. 'Or do you want to bail out with the civilians too?'

'Hey,' objected the young American. 'No way. You know me better than that, man.'

Spenser looked at him for a second. 'Sure I do,' he said apologetically. 'I think I must've been awake too long.'

'We could all use some rest,' said O'Rourke. 'But not until the colonel's safe.'

'I'm not leaving,' said McGough.

'Yes you are,' said O'Rourke firmly. 'I'm in charge here, and what I say goes. Fowler, get over here.'

The rig boss did as he was told.

'You and the lieutenant here, get your people onto the escape boats, and go,' ordered O'Rourke. 'We've got some serious problems of our own to sort out.' He filled Fowler in.

'I'm sorry about the colonel,' said Fowler when O'Rourke was finished. 'He's a brave man.'

'I know,' said O'Rourke. 'Now, these boats of yours. Do they have radios?'

'Low-range.'

'The lieutenant will contact the sub on their frequency, right?'

McGough nodded reluctantly. 'I don't . . .'

'No arguments. We need you to be in charge of the boats and tell your commander what's happening here, in case it all goes wrong.'

'But Spenser couldn't get through on the chopper radio . . .'

'Deal with it,' said O'Rourke. He didn't have the time or the inclination to worry about what would happen to McGough and the crew after they left the rig. Their fate, like the fate of the men under his command, was in the lap of the gods.

'OK,' said McGough. 'What about him?' He gestured in the direction of Conway.

'He stays with us. He may come in useful as a bargaining tool, although I doubt it. But if we have to be blown to smithereens, we might as well take him with us. And he can fly the chopper, if we ever get a chance to use it.'

Conway, overhearing, looked even more depressed about his fate than he had earlier, but he said nothing. He could tell by the set of O'Rourke's face, and those of the rest of the mercenaries, that there was no point in arguing.

McGough nodded, and Fowler gathered his men around him, and told them what was happening. There were some murmurs of dissent from the crew when they found out that they were abandoning the rig, but Fowler soon shushed them. Before they left the cinema, he went over to O'Rourke and the rest who were staying, and solemnly shook hands with each of them. 'Thank you,' he said. 'We're obliged.'

McGough said nothing.

'No worries,' said O'Rourke, and Fowler left the room with McGough and the crew.

After they'd gone, Angel said: 'We could've used some of those guys. They're hard nuts. We've got extra guns. And letting McGough go leaves us a man short.'

'No,' said O'Rourke. 'They're tough all right, but they're not pros. And we need McGough to look after them. That's his gig. We can handle this ourselves, or it can't be handled.'

'You're the boss,' said Angel.

'For my sins,' replied O'Rourke.

20

When Willis left the cinema, he went straight to the chopper and switched on the radio. He tuned into a frequency that the commander had given only to him before he left, and spoke into the microphone. 'Bluebird to Exodus. Come in, please. Over.'

He pressed the switch and heard only the distant whisper of static and tried again. This time he got a response. 'Exodus to Bluebird. Exodus to Bluebird. Receiving you strength nine. Come in. Over.'

'Bluebird to Exodus. Get me the commander. Over.'

'The captain speaking, Bluebird,' came the reply. 'Talk to me. Over.'

Willis ran through everything that had happened since Valin and his men had landed on the platform, including the loss of the two MPs.

'Casualties of war,' said the commander of the submarine. 'How's McGough? And your own health? Over.'

'McGough's fine. And I'm not too bad myself,' said Willis. 'My arm's giving me some gyp. But

240

I'm not sure that it's really broken. Just badly sprained. Over'

'Good news. What now? Over.'

'Now we evacuate the civilian crew. I'll get off with them and leave the others behind. I doubt whether they're going to leave without their precious colonel anyway. But I intend to give them no choice. Over.'

'It's a death sentence, Bluebird,' said the captain. 'Over.'

'Which is exactly what my orders were. Over.'

'Then make sure McGough comes out with you. You may well lose the rig. Over.'

'That's not my concern, but I'll keep your lieutenant safe. Over.'

'Good. Do you know what time the charges are set to go off? Over.'

'No. But I imagine it'll be around dawn tomorrow – if you can call what happens out here dawn. Over.'

'Understood, Bluebird. I'll pass your intelligence on, and we'll prepare to take you, McGough, and the civilians on board when you arrive. Over.'

'Thank you, Exodus. I won't be making any more transmissions from now on unless I can find another radio. Over and out.'

When Willis had switched off, he took the front panel off the radio and dug around in the works with his knife until he was satisfied it was beyond repair. Then he replaced the front and went back inside the rig. He made straight for the radio shack, and checked it out. He would be quite satisfied if Jost blew the rig with everyone on board, as long as he had a chance to get off first.

Then he went outside again, just in time to witness the pontoons leaving the platform. He watched as half a dozen, brightly coloured rubber rafts swung out from under the platform into the full strength of the sea, and cursed to himself.

Shit, he thought. That's torn it. He climbed down the metal companion-way until he came to where the pontoons had been hanging underneath the platform. There was one of the rubber boats still hanging from its davits. McGough and Fowler were standing beside it. 'What's the problem?' said Willis softly, and both men spun round.

'Christ, you gave me a start,' said McGough.

'Sorry. What's the problem?'

'No problem,' said Fowler. 'Only I'm not going. I can't just leave the platform. I've spent too long here to just abandon it like that. The rest of the men will be picked up, won't they?'

'I expect so,' said Willis.

'He knows what our orders are, but he won't budge,' said McGough. 'And I can hardly shoot him, now can I?'

'Maybe you can't,' replied Willis, 'but I can.' And he pointed his Scorpion at the lieutenant and the rig boss and pulled the trigger. The force of the first burst took McGough in the midriff and he was sent, arms flailing, over the edge of the platform. Fowler had no time to speak before the second volley cut him down where he stood. Willis pushed him with his foot, and he joined the lieutenant in the sea. The killer didn't bother to look over the balcony. There would be nothing to see through the falling snow. Instead, he climbed on board the pontoon and looked round. Above his head was a bright-red rip-cord, and he now knew how he intended to make his escape.

He climbed out again and made his way back to the closest entrance to the platform, and from there back to the cinema.

'Any luck?' said O'Rourke when he walked in.

Willis shook his head. 'The bloody thing's dead.'

'What?' said Spenser.

'Wrecked. Jost must've seen us hanging around the chopper and got on board and sabotaged it.'

'Are you sure?' said Spenser suspiciously.

'Sure I'm sure. The radio's fucked, and that's all there is to it.'

'Are you sure it wasn't you that did it?' said Spenser. And then to O'Rourke: 'You should never have let this guy go alone.'

'I'm telling you it wasn't me,' said Willis. 'Hell, I don't want to be blown out of the water any more than you do, do I?'

'It's too late for all that now,' said O'Rourke,

inwardly cursing himself for his lack of judgement. 'Just don't go off on your own again.'

'I won't,' said Willis. 'Where are the civilians?'

'Gone,' said O'Rourke. 'And now we've got to get the colonel out.'

21

So there they were, the remains of Valin's squad, in the cinema on Alpha Bravo Discovery. Four men and one woman, armed and extremely dangerous. One of them a traitor to the rest, serving his real masters in Whitehall, and determined to see all his companions dead. And they had a single prisoner.

Up in the control tower, their leader was being held by a madman who could blow the whole platform into the icy water in a split second, with a single touch.

'We've got to separate that guy from his detonators,' said O'Rourke.

'That'll be easier said than done,' said Spenser.

'Maybe. Maybe not.'

'So what do you suggest?' put in Angel.

'I suggest we do a recce up there. Now listen. We've got to convince him we've gone, so that he comes out of his hidey-hole. Make him think it's safe. So I suggest that only two of us get close to the radio room. The rest stay well back out of sight. I'll go with Angel. The rest of you stay here, and we'll report back. Everyone OK with that?'

There were no dissenting voices.

Jost and the colonel had watched the civilians leave
the rig too. High up next to the control tower, in
the teeth of the storm, Valin with his hands trussed
behind his back and still under the muzzle of Jost's
automatic, they had peered through the falling
snow as the pontoons pulled out from under the
platform.

'Just you and me now, eh, Colonel?' said Jost
triumphantly.

'If you say so,' replied Valin, his words almost
lost in the keening wind. But he knew better.

'Back inside,' said Jost, grabbing Valin by the arm
and pushing him inside the platform again, so that
he neither saw nor heard anything of the incident
between Willis, Fowler and McGough.

As soon as they were back inside the radio room
again, Jost called up Aberdeen on the radio.

'I have total control of the rig again,' he informed
Conroy, who was still maintaining his vigil by the
radio. 'All other personnel have left the platform.'

'By what method? Over,' asked Conroy.

'By the escape pontoons, which I left operational.'

'Well, thank you for that at least. Over.'

'I have never had any argument with the workers
here. They were just unfortunate to be in the
wrong place at the wrong time. I believe there is
a submarine in the vicinity. Perhaps they should be

informed that there are fifty or more men looking for them. I don't give them much chance unless they are picked up out of the sea quickly. The weather is still bad out here.'

'What about the rig? Over,' asked Conroy.

'Nothing has changed. The charges are still set, and will go off tomorrow morning.'

'What time? Over.'

'Ten hundred hours. Dawn.'

'Will you not reconsider, Mr Jost? We could still pay your demands. Over.'

'It is too late for that. My orders were disobeyed. My men are all dead. And I am tired of fighting. I intend to go out in a blaze of glory, with a noise that will echo around the world, and inspire my comrades wherever they are, to continue their battle against capitalism until it is brought to its knees once and for all.'

Pompous idiot, thought Conroy, but said: 'There must be another way . . .'

But Jost cut him off.

'You're quite mad, you know that, don't you?' said Valin calmly. He was sure that his men were still on the rig, desperately looking for a way to free him and get off safely before the charges blew. And he wanted to lull Jost into a false sense of security. Maintain a dialogue, he decided, so that O'Rourke and the others were allowed to move around freely.

'In your eyes perhaps, Colonel. But in many people's eyes you would be mad too. Crazy as a coot. Is that not the expression? But you and I are not that different, are we?'

'I believe that what I and my men do is for the greater good.'

'The greater good. What a hollow, bourgeois expression. You are a freebooter, Colonel. A mercenary. A soldier of fortune who will sell his loyalty to the highest bidder, until the cash runs out, and you not far behind it. At least my companions and I had a cause.'

'A cause that demanded a lot of money.'

'We all need money, Colonel. Surely you would be the first to admit that. We both use our skills to live. You sell yours to governments, and I hold them to ransom with mine. It is ironic, is it not, that we will both be here together at the moment of our deaths. This time on opposing sides, but who knows, in a different world we might have been allies.'

'Perhaps. But I have no intention of dying quite yet, Jost.'

'You have no choice.'

'Is that so?'

'Yes. I am in command here, and sadly for you, what I say goes.'

'I wonder.'

'Don't make me angry, Colonel. Otherwise' – he looked at the detonator box that was never out of his arm's reach – 'I may show you sooner than you think.'

248

'And spoil our interesting conversation. That would be a shame.'

'Wouldn't it? Now I feel hungry. How about you and I go to the kitchen and prepare a final meal? I'm sure we could find something to tempt us. What do you say?'

Perfect, thought Valin. A chance to get him outside.

'What a good idea,' he said. 'I'm feeling somewhat peckish myself.'

Jost picked up the detonator box and slung it over his shoulder by its strap, and still with the Uzi automatic in his right hand, he gestured for Valin to get up. 'Forgive me if I don't untie you, Colonel,' he said. 'But I think it is wiser if I have you at a disadvantage. Even though we are supposedly alone on board, who knows what little surprises may await us outside.'

Yes, thought Valin. Who knows?

On their way to recce the radio room, O'Rourke and Angel came across a little surprise of their own.

They were passing a darkened room when they both heard a slight noise, like the scrape of a rubber sole on composition flooring. As one they dived for cover, and brought up their silenced automatic weapons ready to fire. 'Whoever's in there better come out now,' said O'Rourke through clenched teeth. 'Or you're mincemeat.'

There was no response for a moment, and O'Rourke repeated his order, underlining the threat by cocking his Scorpion, the sound of the action loud in the silence of the corridor.

After another few seconds a voice said: 'Don't shoot. Please.'

'Come out, then,' Angel said. 'And keep your hands in sight.'

The door to the room opened wider, and a young man appeared, dressed in NP overalls. His hands were at waist height and extended.

'Who the hell are you?' said O'Rourke. 'The company mascot?'

'My name's Jim Clarke,' said the young man. 'I was in the cinema with the rest. I'm waiting for Mr Fowler.'

'What?' said O'Rourke. 'He left the rig an hour ago.'

'No,' said Clarke. 'He said he'd stay. Said he couldn't just leave the place to be blown up without trying to stop it.'

O'Rourke looked at Angel with a mystified expression. 'And what were you going to do?'

'I was going to help him. He's been good to me, has Mr Fowler. I couldn't leave him on his own. He said you'd make us go if you knew, so he was going to get the rest of the lads off, then come and find me, and we'd find you.'

'Listen, son,' said O'Rourke. 'I don't know what's going on here. But there's no one else left on the platform but us, a couple of our mates in the cinema, and our guv'nor upstairs with the loony who's threatening to kill the lot of us. He thinks we've gone too, and they're the only two left. Believe me, your boss isn't here.'

'He wouldn't go and leave me here alone,' said Clarke firmly. 'There's no way. He just wouldn't do it.'

'Let's go and have a look, then,' said Angel. 'Show us where these boats were stored.'

The three of them went down to the floor of the platform, then out into the storm, down the metal companion-way where Willis had walked some time earlier. Like him, they too found the single pontoon hanging from its davits.

'See,' said Clarke, shivering in the cold. 'There's still one here.'

'But no sign of your boss,' said O'Rourke.

'Do you think Jost's got him?' asked Angel. 'And what about McGough?'

'Christ knows.'

'Fuck this,' said the American. 'The last thing we need is some maverick wandering around the rig on his own. If Jost sees him he might blow the whistle on all of us.'

'I don't think so,' said O'Rourke, who had gone to the edge of the platform to look down at the waves below. 'Look.'

Angel and Clarke joined him, and he pointed out some pink spots of frozen liquid on the handrail.

'What does that look like?' he asked.

'Blood,' said Angel, rubbing his gloved hand on it. 'And fairly fresh too.'

'Yes,' said O'Rourke. 'That's what I thought. Fowler? McGough? What?'

Angel shrugged.

Clarke's face was grim. 'What do you think happened?' he asked.

'Your guess is as good as mine,' said O'Rourke. 'But I think someone nobbled your friend. And in the worst possible way.'

'You think he's dead?' said Clarke, disbelievingly, even in the face of all he'd witnessed over the past few hours.

'Sorry, son,' said O'Rourke, putting a hand on the younger man's shoulder. 'But I wouldn't be surprised.'

'But who did it?' asked Clarke

'That's just what I'm asking myself,' said O'Rourke. 'Come on, let's go back to the others.'

And so the two mercenaries missed a golden opportunity to nail Jost, as he and the colonel left the radio room to go downstairs to the kitchen.

When the trio got back to the cinema, and reported what had been going on, Spenser looked at Willis and said: 'Do you know anything about this?'

'Why the hell is it always me?' Willis complained bitterly.

252

'Because you're always missing, on your own, when something goes down.'

'Shit,' said Willis in reply. 'I feel like the whipping-boy here. Jost must've realized what was going on and gone down to check, caught the guy coming back and killed him.'

'Shut up, both of you,' interrupted O'Rourke. 'Nothing's going to be resolved by arguing like this. We might never know. But at least we've got one boat to get us out of here, if we can't use the chopper. All we have to do is get the colonel. He'll know if Jost killed Fowler. We'll sort it out later. We've got more important things to worry about right now. Understood?'

Spenser and Willis nodded, if reluctantly, and Willis made a mental note of what O'Rourke had said about Valin. As far as he was concerned, there was no way now that the colonel could be allowed to be taken from Jost alive.

In the huge kitchen that had serviced the rig, just one floor above where the heated discussion was going on in the cinema, Jost had prepared a scratch meal for himself and the colonel.

'I can't eat, trussed up like this,' said Valin. 'Are you going to untie me, or feed me like a baby?'

'I'll release you if you give me your word as an officer that you'll make no attempt to escape,' replied the German.

After a moment's thought, Valin said: 'You have

253

my word,' and Jost loosened the knots that fastened the colonel's wrists behind his back, and Valin massaged some life back into his dead fingers. 'Thank you,' he said.

They dined on cold-meat sandwiches, doughnuts and coffee, and after their meal, eaten standing at one of the massive, metal tables that dominated the room, Jost lit a cigarette and said: 'The last lap, I think, Colonel. We'll go back upstairs now, and prepare ourselves for death.'

'Melodramatic stuff and nonsense,' said Valin, and threw the dregs of his coffee into Jost's face, and took off in the direction of the kitchen door, which led into the canteen.

'You bastard,' screamed Jost, as he clawed at his eyes with one hand, while the other scrambled for the Uzi that he had put on top of one of the ovens. 'You gave me your word.'

'I lied,' retorted Valin as he hit the door full tilt and disappeared into the darkness beyond, just in front of the first of Jost's bullets, which chewed into the door-frame at his shoulder.

In the cinema, the mercenaries, Clarke and Conway heard the shots from above, and O'Rourke yelled: 'Move it. Something's happening. Angel, stay here with Conway and Clarke. The rest of you follow me.' Then he headed for the door, gun up and ready to fire.

The three men and the lone woman tore along the corridor to the stairs leading upwards and took them two or three at a time. They reached the top of the stairs, just in time to see the far door of the canteen swing shut behind Jost as he pursed Valin. O'Rourke, who was still in the lead, fired a burst at the German's retreating back, but misaimed, and the bullets went high and to the right, tearing chunks out of the wall beside him. Jost turned and snapped off an answering burst from the Uzi, forcing O'Rourke and the others to drop to the floor.

Valin smiled grimly to himself as he kept running. I knew they wouldn't leave me, he thought, as he made for the further flight of stairs up to the control tower, where he knew he would find a weapon of his own. Now we'll see who has the strongest nerves.

Valin burst through the door of the radio room, slammed it shut and threw the locks, just a few vital seconds before Jost reached the top of the stairs behind him and emptied the last of the magazine of his automatic into the door panels, tearing great chunks from the wood, and sending the powerful bullets ricocheting around the interior, forcing Valin to roll under the radio table for safety.

Outside, Jost heard the sound of his pursuers on the stairs behind him, mouthed a curse in his native tongue, replaced the empty clip with one of the half a dozen full ones he carried in the pocket of his thick jacket, adjusted the strap of the detonator box that

255

was still slung over his shoulder, and made for the nearest exit to the outside of the rig.

Inside the room, Valin waited a few seconds for more gunfire, then rolled out from under the table and picked up the Ingram Model 10 sub-machine-gun that Jost had left lying next to the radio, and checked the clip. It was full.

He smiled to himself, went to the door, slipped the lock, and dropped prone to the floor as he pulled it open wide. There was no response from outside, and he stuck his head out into the corridor just as O'Rourke peered over the top step.

'Colonel,' he said. 'Good to see you. Where's the Kraut?'

'God knows,' replied Valin. 'I thought he might be with you.'

'He must've gone outside,' said O'Rourke. 'Has he still got the detonators?'

'Yes.'

'Jesus,' said O'Rourke. 'We'd better get off this thing as fast as we can, before he blows it to hell.'

'Good idea,' said Valin. 'But how do you propose we do that?'

'There's a pontoon down below, fuelled up and ready. I think there's just about enough room for all of us. We can't use the chopper in this weather, although we've captured the pilot. Angel's got him downstairs in the cinema.'

'That was a good move,' said Valin. 'And I think you're right. Discretion is certainly the better part of valour in this case. A discreet withdrawal is certainly the best option. That is, if Jost lets us.'

'With any luck he won't know about it until we're gone,' said O'Rourke. 'Let's move.'

As O'Rourke turned round to go back downstairs, he saw that Willis, who had been bringing up the rear, was no longer with them.

'Where's Willis?' he said.

Spenser looked at Carmen, who shrugged. 'God knows,' said the American. 'He was right there a minute ago.'

'He's gone again,' said O'Rourke. Then to Valin: 'Did you know that the civilians had left the rig?'

'Yes,' replied the colonel. 'Jost and I watched them go.'

'Did Jost kill Fowler, the rig boss?'

Valin looked puzzled. 'What? When?'

'Just after the other workers left.'

'No.'

'Are you sure, Colonel.'

'Sure I'm sure. We've been together since I surrendered to him, until I managed to escape just now.'

'It *was* Willis,' said O'Rourke. 'And that damn pontoon's waiting for him, all primed and ready to go. Come on, let's get after the sod.'

'I knew it was that bastard all along,' said Spenser, as they started off at a run.

'Save your breath,' snapped O'Rourke. 'We'd better move fast, or it'll be too late.'

But it wasn't. As they discovered when they hit the darkness outside, and heard the sound of Jost's automatic, and the burble of answering fire from Willis's suppressed Scorpion.

'The bastard's found Jost,' said O'Rourke as he slithered to a halt in the thick snow.

'Or Jost's found *him*,' said Valin as he stopped beside him. 'Either way, it's stopped either of them getting off the rig in that pontoon.'

Quietly, they climbed down the companion-way, until they could ascertain exactly what was happening. Valin held up his hand, and pulled down his clenched fist in the signal for them to halt, when he saw the flames from Willis's Scorpion just below him, where the Englishman was taking cover behind one of the girders that supported the massive weight of the platform above.

Then, when he heard the harsh bark of the Uzi, and saw the muzzle flash from it, Valin spotted the position of the German beside the great drill that sliced down into the ocean floor, thousands of feet below.

'Got them,' he whispered in O'Rourke's ear, when the younger man slid up beside him.

'Yeah.' O'Rourke had seen them too. 'The pontoon's not far from Jost's position. Maybe twenty feet below him. I don't know if he knows it's there.'

'Understood,' said Valin. 'But we can't let this go on. If Willis gets in a lucky shot, Jost'll blow the rig.'

'And Willis can't get away while Jost's still there.'

'Stalemate. Do you reckon we can get a kill shot at Willis?'

'Not without letting Jost know we're here.'

'I'll go down and deal with him, then,' said O'Rourke. 'I owe the fucker one.'

'Be my guest,' said Valin. 'But watch yourself.'

'He won't even know I'm there,' said O'Rourke confidently.

And he didn't.

O'Rourke shouldered his Scorpion, undid the flap of the holster around his waist, slid down the rest of the companion-way, and crept up behind Willis, who was so busy changing the magazine on his Scorpion that he didn't realize he had company until the lieutenant put the muzzle of his Colt automatic close to the skin at the back of his neck. 'Freeze,' said O'Rourke. 'Or you're dead meat.'

Willis stiffened, but apart from that, didn't move.

'Lay down the gun quietly,' ordered O'Rourke. 'And no tricks. This time I know what you've been up to.'

'I . . . I . . .' stammered Willis.

'Shut it,' said O'Rourke. 'I'm tired of listening to you and your excuses. I don't know what you've been playing at, but as of now it's over.'

Willis didn't say another word, but just obeyed

O'Rourke's order, laying down his Scorpion in front of him.

'Put your hands above your head, and move back towards . . .' said O'Rourke. He was interrupted by the boom from Jost's Uzi, and the clang and screech as the bullet hit the girder close by him and Willis and flew off into the storm. As O'Rourke involuntarily ducked, Willis seized his chance and threw himself back at the lieutenant, knocking him to the floor, his Colt sliding across the top of the caked snow to disappear into the darkness.

Willis rolled round on top of O'Rourke, and slammed his head back against the metal of the floor, once, twice, three times. O'Rourke felt himself losing consciousness, but he managed to bring his right knee up into Willis's chest and break the hold he had on his head. Willis attacked again, but O'Rourke, remembering the injury to the other man's right arm, grabbed it with both hands and twisted hard. Willis screamed with pain, and scrabbled with his left hand at the scabbard on his hip, desperately trying to draw the Randall No. 1 and finish the fight. His hand found the knife, and as he came up to give himself the room to plunge it into O'Rourke's chest, Jost spotted him, aimed carefully and fired the Uzi. The heavy-calibre bullet from the Israeli pistol hit Willis in the back, high and to the left, tearing through vital organs, ripping a hole in his heart and killing him instantly, before exiting through the front of his chest, spraying O'Rourke with chunks of meat from his body and shreds of material from his clothes.

In the faint light that filtered down from the platform above, O'Rourke saw the startled expression form on Willis's face, and the spout of blood spew from his mouth, as he collapsed to the ground.

O'Rourke pushed Willis's body aside, grabbed his Scorpion, and fired a short burst which sent the German scuttling back to cover. Then the lieutenant dashed up to join Valin, Spenser and Carmen.

'Willis copped it,' he said breathlessly. 'Jost got him, just before *he* almost got me.'

Before Valin could reply, Jost screamed through the sound of the wind. 'You bloody fools. I warned you what would happen if you crossed me, didn't I?'

'Relax,' Valin shouted back. 'We only came to deal with our own man. He's dead now. This is a stand-off. Let us leave the rig, and we'll give you no more trouble.'

'This is no stand-off,' screamed Jost in reply. 'I still have the detonators, don't forget. Now back off, or I'll kill us all.'

'Shit,' said Valin to his companions. 'Come on, let's get back inside. We're wasting our time here.'

Once again they returned to the cinema.

'What's going on?' asked Angel, as soon as they got through the door.

Valin told him.

'So Willis *was* double-crossing us?' he said, when the colonel had finished.

'Looks like it,' said O'Rourke. 'I should've realized sooner. I screwed up.'

'Don't worry about it,' said Valin. 'Everyone makes mistakes.'

'But why was he doing it?' asked Angel. 'Why try and screw us, when we were working for his boss?'

'That's something we'll have to find out when we get back and talk to Bryant-Marshall,' said Valin grimly.

'*If* we get back,' said Spenser.

'Why don't we talk to him now?' asked Carmen. 'Can't we get into the radio room?'

'You're a marvel, Carmen,' said Valin. 'Why didn't anyone else think of that? Come on, the lot of you. Let's go and make contact with our paymaster and find out what the hell is going on.'

But it was not to be. Just as they all crept up the stairs towards the control tower, the mercenaries with guns at the ready, an explosion shook the building around them, and an emergency klaxon began to wail.

'Christ, he's started,' whimpered Conway.

And then the phone inside the radio room began to ring.

Valin ran up the rest of the flight, through the door, and grabbed the receiver off the hook. ' thought you might be there,' said Jost. 'That wa the radio mast, just in case you were thinking of calling anyone.'

The bastard read our minds, thought Valin, but said nothing.

'Just another eleven to go,' said Jost. 'Now I don't know how many of you there are, so I'm not going to ask you to surrender, or anything stupid like that. I wouldn't know what to do with you if you did. Except kill you, of course. No. I'm going to enjoy the next few hours, Colonel. You'd better make sure you stay well away from the charges I've set, because until the deadline of dawn tomorrow you're never going to know which one will go off next. I hope you've found them all, because life can be full of surprises.' And he hung up.

'Bastard,' said Valin. 'How many of those damn things did we find?'

'Nine,' replied Clarke.

'Christ. So that means there's three we don't know about. Could be just our luck to be blown up by some surprise package.'

'Two,' interrupted Clarke authoritatively. 'I was on the sweep teams with Fowler. We didn't come up this far – we missed the one that just went off. And shouldn't we check the site of that explosion? If this rig catches fire, we'll be dead anyway. Bombs or no bombs.'

'Good man,' said Valin. 'I think we'll have to treat young Mr Clarke here as our authority on the rig from now on. Right, let's see what damage has been done. And can you turn off that damn siren?'

Clarke grinned for the first time. 'Sure. This way.'

They all went up into the control tower, and Clarke switched off the scream of the klaxon, then they investigated the explosion. There was no fire, as the charge had been a small one intended to knock out just the aerial and cause little other damage.

'He thought of everything,' mused Valin. 'And there's damn all we can do about it.'

'Not quite,' said Clarke. 'Did you say he was down by the drill?'

'Yes,' said Valin.

'Then I can blow the sod away,' said Clarke. 'If he's in the right spot at the right time.'

'How?' said Valin.

'Easy,' replied Clarke. 'This morning we weren't pumping. We closed down the well. But the oil down there is under a hell of a lot of pressure. When we start pumping again, we bring it up slow. But if I release all the valves at once, that gusher will come in at maximum force. The whole thing will blow wild – and most of the drilling equipment will go up with it too. Anyone close to that part of the platform just won't know what hit him. He won't have a second to set off the charges.'

'Isn't that kind of dangerous?' asked Spenser.

'Not as dangerous as waiting for that bastard to blow us into the water,' replied Clarke.

'How come you know so much?' asked Spenser. 'You don't look any more than sixteen.'

'Twenty-two actually,' said Clarke. 'And it's my job. I'm not going to be a roughneck all my life. I want to be a rig boss like Mr Fowler – like he was, I mean. And he was bloody good at it. The blokes used to call me his shadow. I was always following him around. Learning, like. He taught me a lot. And the first thing you learn is what can go wrong on a rig like this. It's no picnic, believe me, out here for weeks on end. You've got to know what's the worst that can happen, how to stop it, and once in a while how to start it. There'll be damage to the rig all right, but it won't break. Trust me.'

'I think we have to. Go ahead, Mr Clarke,' said Valin.

'Call me Tony. All my friends do,' said Clarke. Together they trooped down through the rig again, until they came to the pump room. Clarke switched on the lights, then studied the various pressure dials that were dotted around the walls.

'Getting pretty hairy,' he said. 'These haven't been monitored since that lot came on board. Could be dangerous.'

'How so?' asked Valin.

'If the pressure builds up too much, the pipes will blow without any help from me. But that makes it all the better. Do you know where he is exactly?'

'He was down on the lower levels, right above where the pontoons were kept.'

'That's good,' said Clarke. 'Perfect. But is he still there now?'

'I'll go and take a shufti,' said O'Rourke. 'Wouldn't want him to miss the party.'

O'Rourke went out on to the framework of the rig and made his way round the edge, keeping as low a profile as possible while peering through the mixture of snow and stinging sleet that was still falling through the darkness.

After a few minutes he was rewarded by the glimpse of a flash of torchlight down by the drilling machinery. O'Rourke smiled a bitter smile as he thought: just like the king checking on his kingdom. He resisted the urge to take a shot at the light, as he knew that the Scorpion he carried was not the gun for sharpshooting, especially with the conditions as they were. So instead he went back to the pump room and gave the rest his status report on Jost's whereabouts.

'Good,' said Clarke, who seemed much older and more mature now that he was in control of the rig's pumping machinery. 'Let's fuck with him. Now, don't worry if it seems like the rig is shaking itself to pieces. It won't.' And with practised skill he began to throw switches and pull levers, before going to the computerized control panel that sat in front of half a dozen or so dead monitor screens. He tapped out a command, and one of the screens winked into life. He scrolled slowly through a continuous list of numbers in white print on a blue background. Then three orange lights blinked on the control panel, and Clarke grinned. 'Emergency,' he said. 'Going to condition orange.' He punched in another command, and two more monitors came on. Then a final one, and the orange lights turned to red, and for a split second, before he killed it by flipping a switch, another klaxon began to howl.

'That's it,' he said, and looked at his watch. 'Give it a minute. Then you'd all better hang on to your hats.'

'Can we watch it?' asked O'Rourke.

'I wouldn't if I were you,' said Clarke. 'It's safer in here, believe me.'

'I just want to see what happens . . . Colonel?' said O'Rourke.

'I'd listen to Tony if I were you,' said Valin.

'But I need to be sure he's dead.'

'Go on then,' said Valin. 'But for Christ's sake, be careful.'

'You know me,' said O'Rourke, and sprinted from the room, back to where he'd spotted the torchlight.

He was just in time. When he got to his vantage-point, all seemed serene. He looked through the now again, and saw for the second time the faint twinkle of a torch. Then suddenly, without any warning, apart from a rumble from below, the whole rig shook, as if touched by the hand of God.

And at first, in what seemed like slow motion bu grew ever faster, the centre of the platform explode upwards and outwards in a spray of thick, blac crude oil.

O'Rourke knew that he should get back inside but he wanted to be sure of Jost's fate. He saw th torch flicker and die, and a scream echoed throug the fearful noise of the machinery being destroyed only for it to be cut off suddenly and finally.

O'Rourke grinned triumphantly. But he ha waited for a split second too long. The balcon on which he was standing began to shake wildly and he clung frantically to the railings, as chunk of metal, some almost the size of small cars, flev by him. Then he was caught in the deluge of oil It covered him from head to foot in a second and the tenuous footing he had on the balcony which by then was writhing like a snake, becam even harder to maintain, as the oil soaked into th thick snow that was banked on it, and his hand slid from the metal rail as they too became covere in the thick, freezing liquid that was being pumpe up from the deep.

He heard rivets pop as the balcony was throw in one last convulsion, the tortured metal gave and he slid downwards. For one horrifying second the black water yawned beneath him, and wit all his strength he grabbed at any handhold h could find, and dug the toes of his boots int the ice.

Just when he thought he was done for, and nothing could stop his fall, his shoulder hit something hard, and he felt his collar-bone snap, but felt no pain, his adrenalin was pumping so hard. The blow spun him round 180 degrees, and he grabbed whatever he'd hit, and wrapped his arms around it tightly. Whatever it was bent under his weight, and he slid further, only to be brought up with a jerk as it held.

As he hung a hundred-odd feet above the North Sea, O'Rourke hardly dared move, as the piece of the platform he was clinging to began to bend slowly away from its base.

The platform was by then still, except for the black ooze that was continuing to pump from the ruptured pipeline.

Then O'Rourke felt himself beginning to slip, and at last the pain of his injury registered, and he stifled a whimper.

Christ, he thought, I should've listened to Clarke. And just as he felt he must relax his hold, and plummet into the freezing water below, a cheery American voice said: 'God almighty, Mark. You look a sight.'

Through stinging eyes, O'Rourke looked upwards, to where Angel was leaning through a hole that had been ripped in the side of the platform, and extending his arm towards him.

22

O'Rourke spat out a mouthful of the gritty oil that filled his mouth, and said through lips burning from its touch: 'Angel. Thank Christ. Get me off here.'

'Doing my best, son,' replied the American. 'Can you give me your hand?'

'I've broken my collar-bone,' said O'Rourke, gingerly extending his left hand. 'Take it easy, will you.'

'Sure,' said Angel, and grasped O'Rourke's hand.

'Shit, you're slippery,' he said through gritted teeth, as he struggled to get a grip.

'Don't take all day,' said O'Rourke. 'Whatever this is I'm hanging on to, it isn't very secure.'

'No problem,' said Angel as he found purchase, and took O'Rourke's weight. 'You'll be up here in a second.'

Hampered by his injury, O'Rourke clung awkwardly to Angel, as inch by inch the American hauled him in, until they both lay breathless inside the body of the platform.

'Thank fuck you came,' said O'Rourke. 'You saved my life.'

'What – again?' said Angel. 'Be sure to remember me in your will.'

'Count on it,' said O'Rourke. 'Where are the rest?'

'Looking for you.'

'Are they OK?'

'Sure. Did you see what happened to Jost?'

O'Rourke grinned briefly, his teeth white in his oil-streaked face. 'Yeah. He copped it.'

'You sure?'

'Course I am.'

'Good. You up to finding the rest?'

'Sure.'

Angel got up, then helped O'Rourke to his feet, and they walked along the corridor, which was tilted at a crazy angle.

'That blow-out did some damage,' remarked Angel.

'Tell me about it,' said O'Rourke. 'I was there, remember?'

'Something to tell your grandchildren.'

'If my balls don't get blown off first.'

And as they turned a corner they saw Valin and the rest heading their way.

'My God, it's one of the tar babies,' said Valin when he saw O'Rourke. 'Looks like you've been in the wars, Mark.'

'I didn't pay attention to what you said,' O'Rourke said to Clarke. 'And I nearly bought it. If it hadn't been for Angel, I'd be deep-sixed by now.'

'Purely my pleasure,' said Angel, touching his forehead in a salute.

'Jost's dead,' said O'Rourke. 'I saw him go.'

'Good,' said Valin. 'But we're not in the clear yet. Those other charges are still set to blow tomorrow at o-ten hundred hours.'

'There's always that pontoon,' said Spenser.

'Not any more,' replied O'Rourke, with a voice laced with pain. 'I saw it being blown into shreds when the gusher blew.'

'Damn,' said Valin. 'Our only hope's the chopper then. We'd better go and see if it's still in one piece. And as they turned yet another corner, the colonel in the lead, they were confronted by the nightmare figure of Jost standing in the shadows, his body as black with oil as O'Rourke's, his clothes in shreds, his left hand severed at the wrist, blood dripping from the stump, his face now completely contorted with madness, and the huge Uzi auto-matic still clenched in his right hand, its barrel pointing directly at Valin's head.

'Stay where you are,' rasped Jost, through lips blistered from the oil he'd swallowed. 'This time I'm going to finish you.'

The mercenaries had been caught unawares, and they did as they were told.

'We meet again,' said Valin calmly, noticing that the detonator box was nowhere to be seen. 'You look as if you've been through the wars too, Herr Jost.'

272

Jost glanced down at himself, lifted up his bloody stump, and smiled a mad smile. 'Yes, Colonel,' he said. 'I'm afraid I've underestimated you all along. But it's never too late to learn. Isn't that what you English say?'

'Something like that,' said Valin.

'But it seems I am going to have the last laugh,' said the German. 'Now, all of you, very slowly lay down your weapons.'

Once again the mercenaries did as they were told.

'Very good,' said Jost. 'At last you're learning.'

'What happened to the detonators?' asked Valin.

'I lost them when the rig blew,' spat Jost. 'I suppose I have you to thank for that.'

'Indirectly,' replied Valin.

'And now you're going to die for your pains,' growled Jost. 'I should have killed you when I first had you.'

'We all make mistakes,' said Valin.

'But I won't make another.'

'Don't count on it.'

'Don't taunt me, Colonel. You only have seconds to live as it is. Do you wish to meet your maker even sooner?'

'I'll take my chances,' said Valin.

'Then so be it.'

Jost pulled the trigger of the Uzi, which was still pointing at Valin's head. The hammer went down on to the bullet, which detonated, and tried to exit through the barrel to blow Valin's skull to smithereens. But the muzzle was so choked with sludge from the gusher, that the explosion blew back, stripping the metal like a banana skin and exploding into Jost's face, killing him instantly.

'Pretty cool, Colonel,' said Angel, looking down at Jost's body. 'Hey, Mark, I thought you said the dude was dead.'

'Just another bad call,' said O'Rourke bitterly. 'Seems like I'm making them all the time these days.'

'You'll get over it,' said Valin. 'Now come on, all of you. Let's go and check out that chopper.'

'Hold on, skipper,' said O'Rourke. 'I've got to do something about this arm of mine.'

'Well, be quick about it,' said Valin impatiently.

O'Rourke pulled off the dirty scarf he was wearing, and with Carmen's help fashioned it into a rough sling. With a look of agony on his face, he forced his right arm into it.

'Sorry, Mark,' said Valin. 'But we've got to get on. Come on, you lot. Upstairs, quick.'

Tired and filthy as they all were, they made their way up to the helipad. Luckily it was well away from the damage site, and the helicopter appeared unharmed.

'Conway,' said Valin. 'Is this thing flyable?'

'Should be,' replied the pilot. 'It seemed OK when I checked it over earlier. But I didn't have a chance to start her up.' He gave Angel a look of undisguised hatred as he spoke. 'But we'll never get it off in this weather.'

'We might have to,' said Valin. 'Looks like it's our only chance.' He glanced at the luminous dial of his watch. 'O-one hundred,' he said. 'Nine hours to go.'

'I'm not flying it,' said Conway. 'It'll be fatal.'

'So will being here when the charges go off.'

'I can't,' said Conway, with a whine in his voice.

'Why not?' said Valin.

'It's . . . It's . . .'

'What, man?'

'I can't. My nerve's gone. The last time I took one of these up it was in weather like this. It crashed. I killed three people. I was drunk. Court-martialled. Cashiered. Why the hell did you think I got mixed up in this crazy scheme?' Conway put his head into his hands and started to sob.

'Jesus,' said Spenser, and drew the Browning from the holster at his side. 'You'll damn well fly it if we tell you to.'

'Don't you understand?' said Conway, looking up, desperation in his eyes. 'I can't see further than the windscreen.'

'You're a chicken-shit bastard,' said Spenser, cocking the pistol.

'Go ahead,' said Conway. 'Shoot me, but I'm not flying that aircraft.'

'Fair enough,' said Spenser, and fired twice, the heavy bullets knocking Conway to the ground, where he lay still.

'For Chrissakes,' said Angel. 'What the hell did you do that for?'

'Well, he did ask me,' said Spenser, reholstering his smoking gun.

'Terrific,' said Angel. 'Where does that leave us now?'

'I can fly the fucker,' said Spenser. 'I learnt in 'Nam.'

'Just as well,' said Angel. 'I think we might be totally fucked if you couldn't.'

'You have a natural grasp of the vernacular, Angel,' said Valin. 'I've always admired you for that.'

'Though I've never flown one of those suckers,' Spenser added more quietly, referring to the Sikorsky.

'Terrific,' said Angel. 'Now you tell us.'

'Can't we do *anything* to stop the explosions,' said Clarke despairingly.

'Tony, you know what the man said,' said Angel. 'And you've seen them. The charges are booby-trapped. We mess with them, and they go straight up.'

'He might've been bluffing,' said Clarke.

'Do you want to be the one to find out?' asked Spenser. 'Because, believe me, I ain't gonna be on this rig when you do.'

'He's right,' said Valin. 'And with the radio mast out, and the one on the chopper smashed, we can't even call up the sub.'

'So it's evacuation in the chopper or nothing,' said Angel. 'If only this weather would improve.'

'That's the problem, Colonel,' said Spenser. 'I can fly the chopper OK. Hell, one's pretty much the same as another. But it's going to be one hell of a risk trying it in this shit. Especially in the dark. Conway was right about that at least.'

'I'm afraid you're going to have to,' said Valin.

'It'll be suicide,' said Spenser.

'So will sitting tight on this platform,' Angel pointed out.

'Can't we wait and see if the weather improves?' said Carmen.

'But when?' said Valin, looking out at the thick snow that was still falling from a black sky.

'Like you said, Colonel,' said Angel. 'We've still got nine hours. Hell, it can't get any worse, and it might improve when it gets a bit lighter.'

'Then we'll wait,' said Spenser firmly. 'I want at least a cat in hell's chance of getting off this rig in one piece. You guys clear the snow off, and I'll go take a look at the controls. It's been a while. Maybe I should've let that bastard Conway live a little longer, just in case something's changed radically in chopper design since I last flew one.'

'When was that?' asked Angel.

''Bout seven years ago.'

'Great,' said Angel, as the tall shape of his fellow-American vanished into the snow in the direction of the helicopter.

Everyone but O'Rourke started knocking the crusted snow off the body of the chopper and the rotors, and when they were finished Spenser joined them and pronounced himself happy with the layout of the controls in the Sikorsky. 'I just want to give it a whirl,' he said. 'Stand back, everyone.' And he went back to the chopper.

After a second, the waiting party heard the whirr of the starter motor, and both sets of rotors began to turn smoothly, sending shards of ice flying. Spenser revved up the engine until the screws whipped round faster than the eye could see, and the whole body of the Sikorsky shook as if it might fly apart, before he allowed the engine to die. He got out of the cockpit, gave a thumbs up and grinned. 'Perfect,' he said. 'It's all down to fate now.'

After that they all mustered in the galley, and Carmen and Angel rustled up coffee and sandwiches, which they ate in the mess hall. From time to time one or other of them would go outside and look at the weather, which continued to be depressingly bad. Then at o-nine hundred hours Angel went outside to stretch his legs.

He was back in a second, and walked over to Valin and whispered in his ear. 'It's stopped snowing,' he said. 'The sky's clearing.'

'What?' said Valin, who jumped up from the table where he was sitting and went outside as well.

Angel had been right. The fierce snow that had been blowing in the gale-force wind for days had ceased, and the wind itself had dropped to not much more than a breeze.

Valin looked up. He could see stars as the cloud cover melted away.

'Christ, we're going to make it,' he said to Angel, as he saw a slight lightening of the sky in the east. 'Get Spenser.' The American ran back into the canteen.

Spenser and Carmen, with Clarke close behind, and Angel bringing up the rear, were with him in a few seconds.

'It's a miracle,' breathed Carmen. 'Just when we needed it.'

'Let's go saddle up,' said Spenser. 'And get off this pile of scrap metal.'

The troops collected their meagre belongings and marched to the Sikorsky. Spenser took his place in the pilot's seat, put on a helmet, and plugged the intercom into the instrument panel in front of him. The rest took their places too, Valin in the co-pilot's seat, and they too put on helmets, and attached themselves to the in-flight communication rig.

'Here goes,' said Spenser, as he flipped down a number of switches, and watched satisfied, as the dials in front of his eyes came to life. Then he thumbed the starter button. The rotor engine caught, then missed, then died altogether. Spenser tried again, with no luck. 'Dammit,' he said. 'Something's wrong.' He reversed the starting procedure, exited from the cockpit, and climbed up towards the engine mounting. Once there, he took off the cover, and with the help of the torch he was carrying began to delve around inside.

Valin looked at his watch. O-nine hundred plus fifteen. 'We're cutting it fine,' he said to no one in particular as Spenser joined them again.

'Fuel-supply problems, I think,' he said. 'Shit! This would happen now. Who knows anything about aero engines?'

Clarke, who by then had removed his helmet, said: 'I do.'

Spenser smiled bleakly. 'I thought you would. Come and give me a hand. And we need some tools.'

Luckily there was a comprehensive tool kit inside the helicopter, and together Spenser and Clarke both went back to check the engine.

The minutes seemed to gallop past, as they worked on the problem, the sky getting lighter, and their deadline of dawn approaching fast.

At o-nine hundred plus fifty-two, they came back, Spenser shrugged, and pulled a hopeful face, and he and Clarke put their helmets back on again. 'Wish us all luck,' said Spenser through the intercom as he went through the preflight checks once more, and hit the starter button again.

The starter motor whined, the rotor engine kicked in, caught, died, caught again, and roared as he eased on the revs until the shell of the chopper shook.

'Yeah,' he said. 'Now come on, baby. You can do it.'

He eased the joystick slightly, and the tone of the engine changed as the Sikorsky lifted slightly off the pad, before bouncing back down again with creaks of complaint from every rivet.

'Jesus,' Angel hissed between clenched teeth. 'Be careful.'

'Sorry, pal,' said Spenser. 'Better luck this time,' and he worked the controls once more, and this time the chopper lifted smoothly and cleared the drilling equipment, before veering off down towards the calm sea.

'Oh God,' screamed Angel, and Spenser laughed.

'Only kidding, son,' Spenser said. 'This is like riding a bike. Once you've done it you never forget. It's all systems go. Welcome back to the world.' And the helicopter soared upwards, as the rim of the cold, winter sun crept over the horizon.

'You bastard,' shouted Angel. 'I think I've wet myself.'

'Look,' said Valin, and pointed towards the port side. A few miles away, the submarine was sitting on top of the oily sea.

'So they did wait,' said Angel.

'Just as well for the rest,' said Valin.

And then, from behind them, came the light of the first explosion from the charges that Jost and Bernais had planted on the rig.

The first shock waves shook the light helicopter,

and forced Spenser to fight with the stick to bring it back under control.

'Jesus,' said Clarke, as he craned his neck through the Plexiglas window to look back. 'That was close.'

First one, then a second, then a third ball of fire blossomed from the rig, and the passengers in the helicopter could clearly see the pieces of drilling gear being tossed into the sea. Then a fourth, much more violent, explosion burst from the centre of the platform as more charges went off, allowing the crew's quarters and control tower to slip off its supporting legs, hang for a moment over the smooth surface of the icy sea, before plunging into it with a splash that must have sent spray a hundred foot into the air.

'Pretty fireworks, Chris,' said Angel. 'Good job you got this crate up when you did.'

Spenser nodded, keeping his eyes straight ahead, and circled the chopper round to watch as the platform sunk beneath the surface, and the waves caused by its bulk radiated away in a circle.

'That's unfortunate,' he said.

'Bit of a disaster really,' said Valin.

'Still think they'll pay us the money they owe us, Colonel?' asked Angel.

'Why not? We did what we were sent to do.'

'Yeah,' said Angel. 'Ain't it always the same? It's a dirty job, but someone's got to do it.'

OTHER TITLES IN SERIES FROM 22 BOOKS

Available now at newsagents and booksellers
or use the order form overleaf

All at £4.99 net

22 Books offers an exciting list of titles in these series. All the books are available from:

Little, Brown and Company (UK) Limited,
PO Box 11,
Falmouth,
Cornwall TR10 9EN.

Alternatively you may fax your order to the above address. Fax number: 0326 376423.

Payments can be made by cheque or postal order (payable to Little, Brown and Company) or by credit card (Visa/Access). Do not send cash or currency. UK customers and BFPO please allow £1.00 for postage and packing for the first book, plus 50p for the second book, plus 30p for each additional book up to a maximum charge of £3.00 (seven books or more). Overseas customers, including customers in Ireland, please allow £2.00 for the first book, plus £1.00 for the second book, plus 50p for each additional book.

NAME (BLOCK LETTERS PLEASE) ....

....

ADDRESS ....

....

....

☐ I enclose my remittance for £_____

☐ I wish to pay by Access/Visa

Card number

Card expiry date
